Echo

By the same author
Broderie Anglaise

VIOLET TREFUSIS

Echo

Translated from the French by Siân Miles
with an introduction by
John Phillips

VIKING

VIKING
Published by the Penguin Group
Viking Penguin, a division of Penguin Books USA Inc.,
375 Hudson Street, New York, New York 10014, U.S.A.
Penguin Books Ltd, 27 Wrights Lane, London W8 5TZ, England
Penguin Books Australia Ltd, Ringwood, Victoria, Australia
Penguin Books Canada Ltd, 2801 John Street,
Markham, Ontario, Canada L3R 1B4
Penguin Books (N.Z.) Ltd, 182–190 Wairau Road,
Auckland 10, New Zealand

Penguin Books Ltd, Registered Offices:
Harmondsworth, Middlesex, England

First American Edition
Published in 1990 by Viking Penguin,
a division of Penguin Books USA Inc.

1 3 5 7 9 10 8 6 4 2

Introduction copyright © John Phillips, 1988
Translation copyright © Methuen London Ltd., 1988
All rights reserved

Originally published in France in 1931 by Librairie Plon, Paris.

LIBRARY OF CONGRESS CATALOGING IN PUBLICATION DATA
Trefusis, Violet Keppel, 1894–1972.
[Echo. English]
Echo/Violet Trefusis; translated from the French by Siân Miles
with an introduction by John Phillips.
p. cm.
ISBN 0-670-83541-2
I. Title.
PQ2639.R3E413   1990
843'.912—dc20   90-50063

Printed in the United States of America
Set in Bembo

Echo

I N T R O D U C T I O N
Violet Trefusis and Scotland,
A Long Love Affair

Violet Trefusis (1894–1972), daughter of Alice Keppel (née Edmonstone) and the Hon. George Keppel, son of the Earl of Albemarle, spent most of her life in France and Italy and was, in the best sense of the word, a 'cosmopolitan'. Yet, at the same time, Scotland and her Scottish heritage were central to her existence and gave a certain 'romantic' colouring to her life, helping to explain her exceptional character.

Her medieval tower at St Loup de Naud, near Paris, resembles certain Scottish castles and it amused her to fresco the walls of the *jardin d'hiver* with idyllic Scottish scenes, a work executed by her friend and co-biographer, Philippe Jullian. An exchange of letters with the appropriate heraldic authority of Scotland had given her the authorization required to wear the Royal Stuart tartan. In 1967, Florence and Edinburgh became twin cities and Violet, draped in her tartan, gave a splendid luncheon for the Lord Provost of Edinburgh at her Florentine villa, l'Ombrellino. For this occasion, a kilted piper performed during the luncheon in the best Balmoral tradition.

Her literary production provides ample proof of her love of Scotland, the 'legendary' Scotland which she insisted was still flourishing. All her life she was fascinated by Mary, Queen of Scots, and a play, *Les Soeurs Enemies* (English version: *My Favourite Enemy*), shows her knowledge of the period and her devotion to the martyred Queen.

Some of the finest passages in her memoir, *Don't Look Round*, concern Scotland. Violet worshipped her beautiful and remarkable mother and Alice Keppel is the key personage in the book:

> My mother was, in many ways, typically Scots.
> Intelligent, downright, devoid of pettiness or prejudice,
> she loved a good argument, especially a political one. Her
> impartiality and sound judgment were proverbial. I
> should think she was one of the most consulted women in
> England. She was certainly one of the funniest.

Above all, it was Duntreath Castle in Stirlingshire, the Edmonstone ancestral home, which appealed to her imagination. Just fifteen miles from Glasgow, which she found 'not without a certain raffish picturesqueness, reminiscent of a drawing by Jacques Callot', Duntreath is situated near the twin hills of Dumfoyne and Dumgoyne, 'a toy castle surrounded by artificial flower beds'.

Don't Look Round also describes a visit to Duntreath by Alice Keppel's great friend, King Edward VII. This is one of the rare references in the memoir to a relationship which had a profound effect on Violet's life.

> On one occasion King Edward came to shoot at
> Duntreath . . . He had a rich German accent and smelt
> deliciously of cigars and *eau de Portugal*. He wore several
> rings set with small *cabochons* and a cigarette-case made of
> ribbed gold by Fabergé no doubt . . .

A fervent royalist, Violet was pleased to regard both HM the Queen and HM the Queen Mother as essentially Scots in character. She frequently spoke with delight of their passion for dancing – 'typically Scottish' – and of how marvellously they danced.

In the summer of 1963, Violet made her last visit to Scotland and, despite her illness and infirmity, it was for her 'a triumph'. Staying with relations and with old friends, the Wemysses, Roseberys, and Airlies, she was happy to glimpse once again the land which most appealed to her imagination and to feel anew the strength of her Scottish ancestry. On 5 August 1963, she wrote to me from Wemyss Castle:

> I have fallen in love with Scotland all over again! This is the most romantic place of all: a pink granite castle overlooking the sea, and facing Holyrood across the Bay. There is a ruin opposite my windows which looks exactly like the last act of *Tristan*. This is where Mary Queen of Scots first met Darnley. The house is filled with priceless French furniture and charming French servants. My host and hostess speak perfect French like all self-respecting Scots . . .

And from Airlie Castle on 12 August:

> This is, without exception, the most romantic place I have ever seen. It is a pink XIIth-century castle built over a precipice 300 feet high. Below is a turbulent little river on the banks of which graze fallow deer. I would give anything for you to see it. I feel really privileged.
> The 'bonnie Airl' and his wife greeted me as though I were their best friend. The chauffeur who drove me here not only refused a tip, but gave me a present!! The Scots have much in common with the Spanish. Far from being miserly, they are madly generous . . .

Endowed with a remarkable gift for languages, Violet Trefusis is one of the very few British writers – Beckford and Wilde also come to mind – who wrote with equal fluency in English and in French. From 1921 she resided in France. *Echo*, her second novel, published in 1931, gave her the opportunity to delineate her native land, Scotland, and the country which she had adopted, France. It would be difficult to imagine two more different milieux than the brilliant jaded world of a sophisticated Parisian *femme du monde* and that of her young Scottish cousins, totally absorbed in the rustic delights of primaeval Scotland. This

9

vision of Scotland is anachronistic: a land of feudal traditions and of a melancholy romantic beauty.

A striking feature of *Echo*, as of the author's subsequent novels, is her delight in dissecting, with verve and humour, the foibles, the nuances, the peculiar characteristics of society in England, Scotland, France, Italy and Spain. Her plots may be slight, but the portraits of representative national 'characters' which emerge from the novels add up to a rich ensemble, displaying rare gifts of perception. The ensemble preserves a panorama of a certain 'Vieille Europe' which has all but vanished and in which Violet Trefusis was an ornament.

Echo turns on the visit to Scotland of the young Parisienne, Sauge. She leaves behind her worldly and very French husband for a *séjour* in the remote castle of her aunt, Lady Balquidder, where she encounters her twin cousins. The twins, brother and sister, are wonderfully savage and remarkably beautiful. Malcolm and Jean thrive like wild beasts in perfect concord with their natural world. Both resent the intrusion of the newcomer. And then something happens. The charm, the seductive femininity of the young Parisienne is irresistible . . .

In the delineation of Sauge's character it is fascinating to discern a self-portrait of the author. A distinctive feature of Violet – often remarked – was her exceptional voice, and in *Echo* we find Sauge endowed with '*une voix mystérieuse, clandestine*', an excellent description of Violet's own voice. Vita Sackville-West's journal, incorporated in *Portrait of a Marriage*, refers to 'my passionate, stormy Violet of today [25 July 1920] speaking to me in that same lovely voice'. And in Virginia Woolf's *Orlando* the portrait of the seductive Sasha comes to mind: 'she talked so enchantingly, so wittily, so wisely'.

Of Sauge, Violet writes:

elle était imprévisible pour ell-même comme pour les autres. Quand elle sortait de sa torpeur, c'était pour tenter des

*experiences dangereuses et solitaires qui aboutiraient fatalement à
un accident quelconque.*★

Indeed this is how Violet liked to imagine herself!

Echo contains a number of the author's favourite aphorisms
including: '*Les absents ont toujours raison*'.†

Also, describing a house she visits, Sauge is struck by a
'*collection de verres anciens*' and a '*grande glace venitienne*', which
recall ornamental details from Violet's *tour* de Saint Loup.
Then in a climactic moment of the novel Sauge 'attacks' the
Russian music from *Petrouchka* on the old piano. Even in the
last years of her life, this poignant music stirred Violet to
frenzy.

Then, finally, the novel ends on a tragic plaintive note,
expressed by that most Scottish incantation:

> For me and my true love
> We'll never meet again . . .

As Sauge holds her breath:

> The very soul of Scotland was revealed to her in that
> sweet, plaintive song and its oft-repeated themes: the
> endless yearnings of northern love, the longings, the
> fateful separations, the exile, the loneliness, the
> heartbreaking dignity of the Stuarts. In vain did she hope
> for a cry of revolt . . .
>> For me and my true love
>> We'll never meet again . . .

And this was also the refrain which pervaded the life of
Violet Trefusis.

John Phillips
Vevey, Switzerland,
1987

★ She was unpredictable, to herself as well as to others. When she did
  come out of her torpor, it would be to try out experiences which were
  dangerous and solitary, and which would inevitably result in some sort
  of accident.

† The absent are always in the right.

CHAPTER ONE

Quietly and with measured tread, the butler moved to and fro, placing wholemeal bread-and-butter, golden, crusty scones, heather-flavoured honey and ginger-bread cake upon the occasional table.

Near the granite fireplace, old Lady Balquidder sat knitting. Her plump hands were covered with freckles which matched the colour of her hair, still auburn, despite her sixty-five years. From time to time, the ale-coloured eyes, beneath their reddened lids, darted a glance at the door. Her whole person flickered like a small but constant flame.

The grandfather clock, lacking mutton-chop whiskers but otherwise tall, grave and precise enough to be the butler's twin, struck five.

The old lady stirred: a tongue flashed chameleon-like over dry lips as she called the butler:

– Sir Malcolm and Miss Jean have not yet returned?
– No, my lady.
– Then do try and find them. Tell them we are ready for tea.

They were never on time, those two. Always off and away. Quite untameable. Ah, *what* a responsibility it was to have taken on the guardianship of these two orphans, as she had done. They were not wicked of course . . . far from it, but the fiery blood of their outlaw ancestors still coursed furiously in their veins. For were they not descendants of the famous barons who never returned to Scotland from their raids across the border without a rich prize, some terrified young girl, perhaps, or some lace-bedecked young lord to serve as the butt of their drunken revelries? The salutary influence of the eighteenth and nineteenth centuries seemed scarcely to have touched this wildest of families. Their dark, primitive minds were still clouded in the mists of mediaeval times . . .

Lady Balquidder, who had been brought up in the disciplined and civilized society of Edinburgh, was constantly irritated either by the total silence, or by the boisterous high spirits of these extraordinary creatures who communicated solely with each other and in a private language utterly devoid of consonants.

A pair of cannibals could not have been more alarming; their aunt had managed to inspire in them a certain respect only by showing them objects the function of which they could not discern. These objects acquired thereby a certain power not unlike the missionary's cigar or the explorer's camera in places where such things can soon turn into objects of worship.

Her opera-glasses, for example, her silver and mother-of-pearl opera-glasses, through which she had viewed the swelling chest of Jean de Reské, and the swaying hips of Madame Calvé – for Lady Balquidder had in the world of music been something of a camp-follower. Whenever great musical events took place there too was her busy, diminutive person to be found. As a small boy, with hands already like hams, Malcolm had touched these opera-glasses with something akin to awe.

Then there was the fan with the Louis XV figures playing blind man's buff, so vividly that one could almost hear their little cries of alarm; and the photograph album, full of grave, yellowing faces.

– Yes, that's Lady Dudley as Diana, Goddess of the
Moon. Look! She's wearing a jewelled crescent moon in

her hair; and that lady there is the Comtesse Jacques de Waru at eighteen – is it possible that such a marvellous creature could exist in this world? The gentleman in the check trousers is the Marquis of Morès, I danced my first cotillion in Paris with him – ah! there's dear Van Rooy, what a handsome Wotan he made at Bayreuth in 1899 . . . And so she went on, page after page.

Jean's particular fetish had been a parasol made of black lace on a pink lining, and with a handle in the shape of a poodle's head. The little girl could hardly take her eyes off it. To her it seemed the very height of elegance. Had it belonged once to a fairy? Or an angel, perhaps? It was hard to imagine such a thing ever coming from this world.

Poor little things . . . Their Aunt Agnes' annoyance faded. In her mind's eye she could see her sister, her beautiful sister, twenty years her junior; Jean and Malcolm's mother. She could visualize her vivid red hair, her jade-green eyes, her Ariel-like grace.

How had she possibly been expected to get along with such a dense and domineering husband as Sir Nigel Mac-Finnish (whom Lady Balquidder, in a temper, had nick-named 'Hunding')? A child herself, this sister had not been able to tolerate her own children. It was the twins, you might say, who drove her off the face of the earth. And initially, their aunt, into whose care they were given, detested them. However, out of duty, and because she had promised her dying sister, she looked after them despite finding them so like their father that they seemed to belong to a different and hostile clan to her own . . .

Instead of those marvellous copper-coloured tresses, here was a mass of frizzy black curls which Lady Balquidder found a poor substitute; little sultana-coloured eyes replaced the pale jade; in the twins all that was left was the fruit and nothing of the flower of their mother's beauty.

Lady Balquidder was so absorbed in her thoughts that she forgot the time. The scones grew cold in their snowy napkin, the clock ticked quietly to itself. Then suddenly, doors began to slam violently. She sat up with a start.

– Ah, here they are! she murmured, beginning to muster in her mind all the remonstrations she would have to make.

The library door burst open as if blown in by a hurricane. Two rough, dirty, windswept individuals covered in scratches and smelling of tweed, sweat and new-mown hay suddenly hurled themselves on the old lady. She cringed beneath the avalanche.

– Good God! My bonnet! Ah! you're hurting me, Malcolm! For heaven's sake, sit down! Jean! Pick up my knitting!

Jean had grabbed a slice of bread-and-butter and taken a huge bite from it.

– Where have you been?

Jean tried to reply but her mouth was full. Her brother, scarcely more polite, was perched on the arm of Lady Balquidder's deep armchair, pouring himself tea from a great height and making it froth like beer. It occurred to neither of them that they might apologize for being late.

– If you want to know where we've been, ask Jean; she planned it all.

Jean's eyes danced beneath her bouncing curls.

– We went up Benmuick – by the cliff side! she said defiantly. Malcolm nearly rolled down to the bottom of the gorge but I held on to him by his braces. We had such fun!
– But you could have been killed, my dears! You know I've forbidden you to climb Benmuick.
– Well yes, when we were fifteen, but we're twenty now and strong as a couple of oxen, as you've often said, teased Jean, flexing her muscles.

16

– It's not a question of strength alone! One false step
and . . .!
– P'raps so. But it was worth it. The view when you get
there!

Each of the twins had a passionate love of their wild
homeland and were constantly entranced by its beauty.
There was not a tree of it that they did not know, not a
single birdsong they could not identify and imitate. It was
the wellspring of their knowledge and their defence against
the world. The little learning inculcated in them by their
Aunt Agnes and the precepts of Edinburgh society were
powerless against natures such as theirs and only a spirit
vaster then their own could influence them. Books were
replaced by the elements, their tutors were the trees and
beasts of the land which alone had taught them all they
knew.

Whenever Lady Balquidder wished to establish contact
with her niece and nephew, she could only do so by means
of the fragile little objects mentioned earlier. In the twins'
eyes, these linked her with the atmosphere of her European
past which they drank in avidly. She became once again the
heroine of the parasol, the genie of the photograph album,
and in her hands, the faded beauties of the past were brought
powerfully to life again.

Replete and silent now, the twins leaned on either side of
the fireplace, smoking forbidden cigarettes. At first glance,
scarcely a hair distinguished one from the other. The eyes
were dull, the profiles regular, somewhat stupidly Alexan-
drian. Malcolm's cleft chin showed bristle and Jean's was
covered with a soft down. Her nose, though roughly the
same type as her brother's, was clearly the finer, the more
aquiline, the more intelligent. Had a coin been struck with
both their profiles on it, Malcolm's would have provided the
background, the foil, against which to put his sister's more
delicate silhouette.

Their expressions now were identical. Each wore the same

sullen look they adopted when temporarily deprived of animals, birds or trees. To them, this was tantamount to being deprived of sight, for they only saw out-of-doors. If asked, they would have been totally incapable of describing the interior of the castle. Yet Malcolm's notebook was crammed full with minutely-drawn sketches of plants and animals, closely observed and complete in every detail. When they came home, bone-weary, it was only to eat and then, immediately afterwards, to go to bed.

Once or twice, Aunt Agnes had insisted that they go with her to Edinburgh. Being under any kind of roof nearly drove them mad; they were shocked, jolted or offended by every passer-by, every motor-car, and as for the deafening, incessant noise of the trams . . .! Aunt Agnes had blushed to have such savages in tow; a couple of mastiffs would have been less of a social embarrassment.

At Glendrocket they could still pass muster – indeed, the kilts they wore were a picturesque part of the place – but at Edinburgh the twins were quite simply grotesque. Malcolm had been instructed by his aunt that whenever he was in her company he should wear trousers. His trousers had been bought when he was sixteen. They now reached mid-calf. As for Jean's wardrobe, it was impossible to find either a tailored suit or an evening dress that would do. Shop assistants would murmur in hushed, regretful tones, that there was no size to fit the young lady, neither in shoes, nor in hats . . . unless one wished to try men's?

The hairdresser's grimace of disgust when requested to 'mow this' had been a picture. Each of Jean's thick locks seemed to possess a life of its own. However hard he tried to subdue them they sprang back as if alive. 'I might as well be cutting heather,' he muttered through clenched teeth. And even in Edinburgh, where the sight of great giants was not uncommon, this strange couple excited curiosity. 'Sigmund and Sieglind, in brown,' a German student had murmured, espying them in Princes Street.

Poor Lady Balquidder's troubles had only just begun. For old Mrs Sellars, her childhood friend, now doyenne of Edinburgh society, had expressed a wish to meet the young Sir Malcolm and his sister. Accordingly, herded in by their guard dog, Lady Balquidder, the twins, dressed stiffly and awkwardly in their new tight clothes, lumbered in like a pair of recalcitrant oxen. Mrs Sellars, hiding a smile and receiving them with the most exquisite courtesy, was met with a stony silence. Yes and no was all she succeeded in drawing from the pair. Suddenly, into the drawing-room, cluttered as it was with delicately balanced teacups and little folding tables, burst Mrs Sellars' spaniel, Master. Jean, who loved animals, jumped up with a cry and, in so doing, knocked over one of the tables, which fell with a crash. The sound of breaking china was followed by an icy silence.

A voice, seemingly from a great distance, spoke:

– My Saxe teacups! Four broken. Never mind. It's quite unimportant.

Jean stood amid the debris of broken china like a giant chick newly hatched from a tiny egg. She saw the scandalized expressions on the faces of the guests, teacups poised midway to their lips, the pool of tea in which her feet were squelching; she saw all this, burst into tears and, turning to her aunt, now stupefied with shame, cried:

– Why did you bring me here? I *begged* you to leave me at home.

Lady Balquidder's final ignominy was to hear in the background the helpless giggles of Sir Malcolm, the heir.

She must face the facts. It was impossible to take these two anywhere. She was too old and frail for such struggles.

One day, she happened to be in the wonderful cakeshop, Mackay's, where pyramids of scones of all descriptions are temptingly arranged in the windows. No fancy nonsense here! Scottish bakers are a steady, honest breed. They would flee in horror, you can be sure, from the daring intricacies of the *millefeuille*, the powdery seductiveness of the *choux à la crème*, from *éclairs* plastered with chocolate, from the wanton wickedness of the *rum baba*; not for them the dangerous, not to say downright immoral *pâtisserie* of their European peers. However, those who find Scottish fare as dull as a woman with no make-up have simply no taste in these matters.

Lady Balquidder entered Mackay's, followed by her niece and nephew, whose eyes shone greedily at the sight of such wonders to eat. Like Attila's hordes attacking Rome, they fell upon them. As she looked at their ecstatic faces, covered with flour, and heard their groans of pleasure, Lady Balquidder understood she need go no further. She would resume her round of social visits. This time she would go alone.

Restored by this brief contact with civilization, she returned to Glendrocket and continued to hope. But to hope for what, exactly, for these twins? For marriage, obviously, but to whom? They had now been living in this kind of splendid isolation for many years. Naturally, Lady Balquidder had neighbours whom she saw, but they were nearly as old as she was and the few young people who deigned to frequent the place for the shooting had nothing in common with her two charges. With elaborate entourages, they charged up and down the mountains while Malcolm and Jean, lying on their bellies in the heather, hurled imprecations.

– Why can't they stay where they belong; the lily-livered idiots? Why do they have to come up here with their filthy stinking cars, throwing rubbish in our rivers, setting our moors on fire? Ugh!

No, it was highly unlikely that either MacFinnish would find a life companion from such as these.

Now, heads lolling and arms relaxed, the *enfants terribles* were fast asleep. With a slight rustle of silk, their aunt rose, moving from one to the other as if to check something. She looked for all the world like a dry, sly little reptile. Asleep, the twins looked even more like the children they still were.

As their warm, regular breathing rose up towards her, Lady Balquidder could not help but sigh. She might have been bending over a cradle . . .

The Anglo-Saxons are not expansive in conversation, preferring as they do to confine any outpourings to their correspondence. But however reticent English discourse may be considered, Scottish is even more so; according to the Scots mere talk is highly suspect and can lead to no good. Behind these closed Scots doors lies a wealth of experience. The Scot lets others prattle on for the sheer pleasure of hearing their silly chatter. Then suddenly, into their idle banter he will inject a single trenchant remark that sets them all by the ears. Happy with the chaos that ensues, he retreats once again into silence. Frugal in all respects, the Scotsman hoards his words too; why waste them on things of no substance, like ephemeral conversation?

The Scotswoman, however, possesses a particularly wise and caustic spirit of her own which contrasts nicely with the sombre background of conjugal silence. In the Scotswoman, every paradox is on view: a lawyer fighting the law-breaker; logic against superstition; mysticism battling against the role of the housewife; Calvinism crashing through the haunts of the great god Pan.

Inside their vast and largely ugly, sprawling castles, with their myriad squinting embrasures and watchtowers, the lives of these women flow gently and monotonously on. It is her own imagination that supplies the Scotswoman with the adventures of life. Caught between two worlds, how could she not prefer the romantic past to the materialistic present? She abandons herself to heroes long since dead. Ivanhoe-like, she stretches out her arms to Rob Roy, and from him moves on to the even wilder embrace of Quentin Durward. For this dreamy adventuress nothing is impossible. While remaining practical in her daily life, and reasonably loving to her husband, she constructs in her mind's eye the most extravagant scenarios, and in her tales nothing is too outrageous to be included. There is nothing in the least neurotic about this tendency; indeed the Scottish woman is more well-balanced than most. Yet she can say quite calmly:

– Last night, when I was getting into bed I saw the cavalier's head on the dressing-table again; that's the third time in two months, pass the salt would you please?

Believe me, you do find yourself in the end being rather impressed by these innocent little understatements. The Scots react with great casualness to any sinister rustlings of mysterious wings, to stories of passionate entanglements and the crime and chaos to which they lead.

In contrast, some perfectly ordinary practical joke can lead to a lifelong feud, and an ordinary game of hide-and-seek can lead to death. Montieth's bride hid herself in an old coffer and her body remained there, undiscovered, for a hundred years. Characters move in and out of two shadowy worlds, wandering at will between the warring camps of Reason and Fantasy and mingling their colours in a rainbow of dreams. When both the real and the imaginary are treated with indifference, the two become indistinguishable. Often it is the truth and not fiction that appears implausible. At any rate, the end result is that Scotland becomes a place too frightening to remain in . . .

Agnes Balquidder's life was no exception. It, too, contained a secret unwritten novel. For thirty years, she had been in love with Paris. This dry little Scotswoman blushed at the mere mention of the Champs-Elysées, and at the slightest reference to the boulevards her heart beat a little faster. The perspicacious old society of Edinburgh had quickly noticed this and concluded that during her youth, spent in the Faubourg Saint-Honoré with her other sister, the Marquise of Bréouge, she had been the cause of one of those ill-fated passions to which the sons of France are somewhat prone.

Since Lady Balquidder could never admit to being in love with an entire city, it was not long before her reactions were differently interpreted. She must have been the mistress of some decrepit old roué of a marquis . . . They had been seen together at the Pré-Catalan, at Versailles . . . It was he who had given her that brooch in the shape of a comet; those letters with the V^c *arrondissement* postmark had been penned by an adulterous hand . . .

So it was that Lady Balquidder acquired the mysterious reputation of a *grande amoureuse* and was much fêted. Whenever she visited her sister, Lady Balquidder's husband became the object of muted sympathy. He was encouraged to get out and enjoy himself, to seek distraction elsewhere. 'What holds you back?' asked other, erring, husbands, assailing his innocent ears with salacious stories and nudging him deeply in the ribs. He lived a long and happy life and died without ever understanding. Agnes' tears were considered hypocritical and her grief excessive. She never returned to Paris again. 'It is obvious she feels guilty,' proclaimed her friends, but her correspondence with her sister continued uninterrupted.

Now this same sister had a daughter who was, by all accounts, ravishing, and she, in turn, was married to a Frenchman, Alain de Cervallon.

Lady Balquidder's feelings, therefore, can easily be imagined when one fine day, she received a letter from Madame de Bréouge. The latter's epistolary style, unchanged since her youth, consisted of a mixture of parenthesis and emphasis.

I am terribly worried, my daughter is unwell; she is slightly neurasthenic (as always at this time of the year) and my son-in-law is also greatly worried. The doctor (our old Dr Lefèvre, who took such good care of you when you had bronchial pneumonia) prescribes a complete change of air. You will probably guess what I am about to ask. It is, indeed, that I should like to send her to you for at least six weeks. Alain will go and take the waters alone; even the most devoted couples need a little rest from each other from time to time and I think that Alain, though he is a perfect husband, is *getting a little bit on her nerves*. Sauge is depressed. What she needs is a change, a good deal of fresh air and to be unhampered, though safe. In other words, she needs to come to Scotland. And this would be a good way for her to get to know her cousins, whom she shows every sign of adoring from a distance. And you, dear Agnes, will find a niece of whom you will not be ashamed, I assure you. Write to me, dear Agnes. I can't wait to know whether this plan is agreeable to you and that you do not think my *very natural* request indiscreet, given the affection which binds us both.

Several times, during the reading of this missive, Lady Balquidder passed her tongue over her lips – for her, a sign of great agitation.

What, she thought, a Parisienne at Glendrocket? A self-assured little princess, used to all the pampering and the luxuries of French high society, let loose on the moors with two silent savages? Lady Balquidder had no illusions about the welcome which would be afforded the newcomer. Indeed, her heart beat a little faster at the mere thought of it.

That evening, after the twins had returned from fishing, she took out the letter and, in a tremulous voice, read it through to them. She waited. The silence was so deep one might have thought the room empty. The tall grandfather cloth ticked in rhythm with her own heart. Suddenly she spoke, in a high voice, full of challenge:

– I think you will make your cousin very welcome. She
has been ill; she needs peace and . . . kindness.

As the silence continued, the fiery nature of the tiny, freckled red-haired old lady rose up, and with it the fury of her youth.

– It's no good sulking like that. It'll get you nowhere
with me . . . Your cousin will come to Glendrocket and

24

if you do not behave courteously towards her, I shall . . .
– You'll what, Aunt Agnes?
– I shall certainly not go away, if that's what you're
thinking! I shall (and here an inspiration) *I shall invite the
entire family!*

This time, her words hit home. There were groans. Jean
was the first to speak. In an expressionless voice she asked:

– And what about us?
– You can do as you please, it makes absolutely no
difference. Now please leave me alone, I have some
letters to write.

Anxious to work out a plan of campaign, the twins needed
no second bidding. As soon as the door was closed, Lady
Balquidder subsided triumphantly into her chair. Why hadn't
she always been like this with them? The future was hers.

Her niece and nephew had very different ideas. Caught
initially off-guard, they had not had time to loosen their
unpractised tongues but now, after many hours of discussion, they were ready to reply. So as not to feel at a
disadvantage in front of the enemy, they had taken care to
wash and appear her equal. Already they look cleaner and
she hasn't even arrived, was Aunt Agnes' immediate
thought, though she kept it strictly to herself. The future
was hers. The twins had agreed that Jean should say nothing
while her brother took a glass of port alone after dinner.

Accordingly, Jean went up to the drawing-room with her
aunt in seemly silence, careful not to upset the situation with
an untimely remark. Malcolm arrived, slightly flushed from
the two glasses he had eventually drunk to bolster his
courage. He installed himself in front of her, his back to the
fire. Lady Balquidder hid a smile. She was beginning to
enjoy herself.

He began to outline all the dangers to which her relative
would be exposing herself if she came to Glendrocket. What

would a person like her, brought up at the very centre of the throbbing life of the metropolis and used to all its thousands of distractions, make of their solitary, uneventful life? What about the loneliness of the place?

—You've asked us to be nice to her, he said, we shall
behave correctly and that is all. You must realize that
with the best will in the world we have very few
common interests. When we've said 'Good morning. Did
you sleep well?' to this stuck up little . . . ('stuck up'
came out unwittingly, since the twins had agreed not to
be insulting) what else can we think of to say? She won't
be interested in our dogs, or our fishing, or our hunting
. . . if it's us you're relying on to keep her company,
she's in for a very lonely time. Besides, the less we see of
her, the better it will be, the more likely we can remain
polite. But if you stick to your decision, there is one
solution that will make everyone happy. Jean and I could
go camping for . . . for the whole time she's here. It's the
time of the year for it; it hasn't rained for three days; we
can take the tent. Out of sight, out of mind. You can't
refuse us that, surely?

Malcolm's speech concluded less elegantly than it began. Never in his life had he made such a long one and now he could remember only two parts, the beginning and the end. There was supposed to have been a middle, but he had no recollection of it. Ah well, too bad. Out of breath, he mopped his brow.

Aunt Agnes had no wish to be softened in her resolve by the sight of the twins' mighty exertions; she had seen Jean's lips move to prompt her brother when he skipped parts . . . Very quickly, in her little mosquito-like voice, she said:

— No, my dears, I absolutely insist that you stay and meet
your cousin. She is only eight years older than you. You
could be good friends; she needs a change; everything
here will have the charm of novelty about it. She can go
with you, walking and shooting . . .

– Not for long, growled Malcolm through clenched
teeth.
– Well, said Lady Balquidder, using her newly discovered
weapon, if you are not pleasant to her, I shall invite not
only Sauge but her husband and my sister also.
– Why not the cook and butler too? said a practically
inaudible voice.
– I beg your pardon?
– Nothing.

The twins collapsed. Never had their little aunt stood up
to them so spiritedly. All their carefully prepared speeches
were to no avail. And the present, disastrous as it was, paled
into insignificance beside the incalculably ghastly prospect
of an entire French family wandering about the moors,
filling the house with their noise and poking their noses into
all the secret places.

No, anything but that. And as for their so-called cousin,
she'd soon see what she was up against. See if they didn't
frighten her off in three days! In the meantime, they lapsed
into a sullen silence which Lady Balquidder would have been
very foolish to take for consent.

Lady Balquidder, however, no longer cared two straws
what her niece and nephew thought. Already in her dream
world she was back in Paris. The Paris of the old days! The
Paris of the chic little broughams and beribboned nannies; a
Paris which Fursy and Fragson had on its knees laughing and
whose social life revolved around Edward VII (had he not
dined twice at her sister's?); the Paris of strolling *boulevardiers*,
of wasp-waisted creations by Worth and by Doucet.

Lady Balquidder allowed herself to sink into a sweet half-
sleep in which she was a guest at the wedding of the *Petite
tonkinoise* and President Loubet . . .

– When I think, continued Malcolm, that in eighteen days
we shall have this silly little halfwit under our feet.
– Yes, agreed Jean, I can't wait to see her teetering about
the moors in Louis Quinze heels. She'll want to have

snails every mealtime – when she's not eating frogs, that is. She'll have a little corncrakey voice, and she'll keep saying '*Ah mon Dieu!*' all the time. And, of course, she'll be fat and dumpy, like her mother; you know, there's a photo of her on Aunt Agnes' desk.

– Well we can certainly make her life a misery, proclaimed Malcolm with relish. We'll take her fishing for perch and insist she puts the minnows on. We'll make her carry dead rabbits . . .

– What if she faints? suggested Jean, in peals of laughter at her brother's plans.

– All the more fun, the perfect gentleman replied, stuffing his mouth full of humbugs.

– Just the same, I'm quite keen to see her, admitted Jean, whose sole feminine attribute to date was a budding curiosity.

– You'll do that soon enough, lamented Malcolm, drawing away. Here, come and help me untangle my lines.

At this very moment, in a certain dining-room in Paris, dinner was coming to an end. The breezes of the summer night drifted through windows flung wide open onto a small, carefully tended garden. The trees were still, as if listening to the conversation. A thin silver crescent moon was caught in the web of their branches like a fish trapped in a net.

– When an incident is closed, it's simply closed, that's all, affirmed Charles-Henri Poncevaux, between puffs of his cigar.

– Speak for yourself, Charles-Henri. All the incidents I know of are ajar, said a lazy voice which lingered, like smoke, on the air. Everyone laughed, firstly at the discomfiture of Charles-Henri, who loved a *bon mot*, and

secondly because the speaker, having taken no part
whatsoever in the discussion till then, seemed half-asleep.
– Sauge, darling, don't let your voice trail off like that,
one day it may not come back, teased her husband.
– It's true, she does have the strangest voice, Charles-
Henri declared, suddenly alert, as if someone had put
everything in a nutshell.
– How would you describe it? asked Villaret, the writer,
for Charles-Henri's lack of imagination was a source of
much amusement to them all.
– Well, you know me, I'm no poet, but it's a . . .
mysterious, a clandestine kind of voice, I'd say.
– I say, I say, I *say*. Well *done*. The voice has worked on
some of us I see!
– She's stopped talking.
– She knows we shouldn't laugh about her voice.
– What a boon to have one like that when one's as lazy as
Sauge!
– She could almost be let off speaking altogether.
– It really is too funny, exclaimed Villaret admiringly. In
her kindness she has dropped us one little sentence since
the fish course and here we all are, mulling over it still,
picking its bones, you might say.

But Sauge was no longer listening. Often her attention
wavered on occasions such as these and, when it did,
everything that happened around her was like a distant street
scene, watched from a window. She tossed out the odd
sentence much like throwing a pebble to a dog. Then, having
forgotten about it completely, she was astonished to find it
faithfully returned.

– It really is silly to try and include her; she's not listening
at all.
– Perhaps she knows us only too well, a voice said, full of
irony.
– I'd just as soon she didn't listen, then we can carry on
talking about her as if she weren't here.

Sauge was genuinely surprised by all the fuss. Why couldn't they leave her in peace? Should she ever have accepted this invitation? It was the garden, of course, that had tempted her to come. In July, it was so lovely to dine in a room giving onto a garden. 'Sauge is in love with the trees as usual,' her husband used to say. She was always the last to arrive at dinner parties and always the first to leave. She spoke as little as possible and paid the minimum of attention to what was said. What a waste of time it all was! Like a prisoner in the dock, she remained silent. Then, when all eyes were upon her, and when, out of guilt, she finally decided to make an utterance, it was like . . . it was like . . . well, what had just happened.

Why did they put up with her? Was it because she was pretty? That couldn't be it, surely? Because she was young? But there were both younger and prettier women so it had to be something else. Wasn't it really because she tended to keep them all in suspense? Because she was as unpredictable to herself as she was to others? If she ever came to arouse herself out of her torpor, it was to drift off into wild and dangerous adventures that would surely one day end in some accident or other. She was friendless, surrounded by a group of acolytes willing enough to applaud all her exploits provided they were not involved. Drawing the assembled attention in around her, like snuggling into a scarf, she said in a steady voice:

– Then it's a good thing I shall be leaving soon for Scotland: I realize that I'm not very good at dinners at the moment.
– When have you ever been? added her husband.
– But what will dinners be without her? Her silence is more powerful than all our little speeches. We are carried away on it, like petals soaked in the flowing waters of the river.
– This would be all very well, chaffed her husband, if Sauge's silences were long-term, but let me tell you one

thing; if any society hostess wanted to write in her little notebook, let's say: 'Charles-Henri Poucevaus, financier, something-in-the-City; Jean Villaret, man of letters, brilliant conversationalist; Sauge de Cervallon, pretty, silent little creature', she would be in for a shock as far as the latter is concerned. There's no bigger chatterbox if she feels like it. And almost anything can set her off; a chance remark, a little comment can make her madly funny; the Fratellini's clowns aren't in it! Isn't that right, Jean? You'll bear me out?
– Yes, I will. I think if this whole thing hadn't started, Sauge would have been the life and soul of the party. It's silence that inspires her, you see; we have nothing to do with the real gaiety that exists within her. It's as mysterious and peculiar as the Indian rope-trick.
– Look here, what on earth have I done wrong? their victim finally exclaimed. God! I shall be glad to get away from all these barbs! How blissful it will be! Oh to be with people who only open their mouths to say 'Pass me the bread'. With sensible English people who prop newspapers up between themselves. 'Too much eloquence is boring,' as Pascal so rightly said.
– Sauge's wish will soon come true. She's leaving on the fifteenth for Scotland, to see her cousins, the MacFinnishes, announced Alain de Cervallon, his voice tinged with sadness. He adored his wife and also understood how necessary it was to conceal that fact, particularly now, as Sauge was yearning for wide open spaces, for fresh air, for a rest cure.

Her husband's last word struck her. MacFinnish. What a shocking mouthful of a name, leaping hideously like a jack-in-the-box into this elegant French conversation. Mac-Finnish! MacFinnish! she repeated with relish, as if the name were taboo. She suddenly wished she need never sit in this delightful, civilized room again, nor be with its elegant and charming guests; not even with Villaret whom she loved like

31

a brother; not even with Charles-Henri, not even with her husband . . .

As she was leaving him, however, she did feel a moment's sadness. How was it she could feel so sweetly disposed towards him now, when only yesterday she had dismissed him as being slightly *passé*. It was because she knew that in a few minutes she would be seeing him no more. There is nothing like a separation to add new lustre to faded relationships. Oh what rubbish, that stuff about absence making the heart grow fonder, she thought, full of contempt for the fickleness of her own emotions. For there were always intervals in her emotional life; short *entr'actes* during which nothing happened. She was tired of loving and her heart was taking a short break.

Used as he was to these periods, Alain de Cervallon still worried, like the owner of some tamed beast at the beginning of the mating season. Would she come back to him this time? He could not even put a name to his vague unease. He had no rival and often wished for the certainty such betrayal would bring, instead of the agony of doubt which accompanied each fresh excursion of his wife's. How far did she go? he wondered. He was beset by a dual and contradictory fear; first, that she was unfaithful to him and secondly, that she was not, and that her love would die as a result, from lack of the necessary stimulus. He might have spared himself this last thought for, once again, as he left her, he was unsure of everything, even of not being loved . . .

The end of July always found Sauge edgy and depressed, very close indeed to the state of total neurasthenia she sometimes entered. She slept badly and was frequently awake when the light of dawn stabbed through the night. The thought of Scotland refreshed her from her fevered dreams like a shower of rain. Green, fresh Scotland, with its deep, melancholy lakes, its dewy moors, its legends and its ghosts . . . This must surely be the country of her dreams, the refuge, the sanctuary in which she would find peace and security. Already her imagination had begun to work on her cousins. Twins, two variations on the same theme, the doubly perfumed fragrance of the same androgynous plant, the voice of youth in harmony.

She knew every other country except this, which in a manner of speaking was her own, and she loved trying to find out how much of a Scot she was. Who, she wondered, did she take after, her father or her mother? From her father, Armand, she would have inherited a certain wickedness, some frivolity and enormous charm. From her mother, aloofness, perhaps, for there was in the latter a streak of puritanism which would never for one moment admit that Armand was not the most virtuous of husbands. Both her parents were united in adoring Sauge and as a result could never quarrel for long. Any mistress's demands were subservient to her merest snuffle. And Madame de Bréouge had only to remind herself that Armand was Sauge's father for any latent irritation to disappear. Now that there were fewer beautiful women around and even fewer who were discreet, domestic harmony was total. And besides loving Margaret, his wife, Armand had for her an almost superstitious respect. It seemed to him somehow that all his good fortune was due to Margaret herself. She was the chain which linked all his treasures, the setting without which they would have seemed less precious. If ever Margaret, tiring of the whole thing, had left him, he was certain all his other ladies would do likewise. Margaret, his silent confidante . . . it was she who, when necessary, could provide him with details of events he himself had long ago forgotten. 'Tell me, when was it exactly I met Germaine de Freylus, was it '93, or '94?' or 'By the way, Adrienne Bernier, when did she and I break up, do you remember?' Margaret remembered everything. She was the only woman in the world who had been able to keep Armand de Bréouge. She remembered that as well.

Not surprisingly, the child had inherited in turn both her father's volubility and her mother's taciturn nature. In the child, her father's cynicism was tempered into irony and her mother's reticence softened to passivity. But there was in her something which neither of her parents had possessed, and that was an insatiable curiosity about human beings. It was a curiosity slightly disconcerting for being totally disinterested. Sauge was careful not to let herself become involved during her frequent excursions into the lives of others. Her curiosity was intuitive; like an enchantress she was able to call up spirits at will, and no terrain seemed too arid for her to conjure from it some new source of information. With the help of what she called her 'divining rod', the driest of characters discovered within themselves unsuspected depths of feeling. The more unpromising her subject, the more assiduously did she apply herself. She confessed to a predilection for lost causes. Alain used to explain: 'Sauge is really nice only to old bores whom everyone else is fed up with,' adding with some annoyance, 'If only it were out of kindness, but on the contrary, it's *pride* that makes her do it. She throws herself into the task of making them less ugly, less boring and the worst of it is that more often than not, she succeeds!'

She restored to every individual the particular and hitherto unrecognized voice that they alone possessed. People who had 'made it' held no interest for her, since no mystery was attached to them. She was bored by a *fait accompli* and, ever since childhood, had been attracted to the unusual.

Her searching curiosity was by now proverbial and she was strong and capable enough to act as a prop to someone who really interested her, as a trellis to the young tendrils of a plant slow to develop.

But whenever the eternally grateful 'subject' showed signs of wanting to stabilize a relationship regarded always by Sauge as temporary, she would quietly slip away, fearful lest a human heart bring her down from the Olympian heights of her disinterestedness.

C H A P T E R   T W O

Lady Balquidder was in an agony of indecision over which room to offer her niece. They were all equally high-ceilinged, equally pale, equally damp, and entirely devoid of comfort or charm. Possessing neither blinds nor shutters, they resembled lidless eyes and the few yards of nondescript material bestowed on them as curtains only heightened the starkness of the atmosphere. The curtains were there merely for form's sake and did nothing either to stop the cold from coming in or the morning sun from searing the eyes of whatever occupant lay in the bed invariably placed opposite.

You could almost go so far as to think that the Scots do not forgive the bed all its voluptuous connotations. Not so far! the beds seem to say. Wicked creatures, wait till we've arranged things our way. Now let's just make this part a little narrower here, this part a little higher. Let's put a little horsehair in this bit, a bit of iron in this. This way, madam! You're not afraid of heights surely? You don't mind cliffs? What's a bit of scaffolding between friends? . . .

Lady Balquidder was more than a little anxious as she contemplated the high, narrow coffin intended for what were the no doubt shapely contours of her Parisian niece. At the far end of the room was a fireplace of carved granite which proclaimed its own close affinity with the tomb.

Really, sighed Lady Balquidder to herself, this room is *most* unattractive. What can I do? One is as bad as the other and at least this room is directly south-facing. The sun, in one of its rare appearances, was already doing its best to warm the craggy chamber. Outside and beyond, the heather-covered moors were as velvety as a Persian carpet.

We don't lack creature comforts, thought Lady Balquidder, not without humour, the trouble is, they are all outdoors . . .

Letter to Alain from Sauge

Between Dover and London
August 13th.

I promised I'd write to you when I arrived but I'm going ahead a little and starting in the train. I wonder what kind of unknown terrain I am entering and, like every explorer worth his salt, I've brought lots of ammunition with me. Like little glass baubles I'm carrying with me precious little stories from home (don't bump into me, I might drop the whole of Paris!).

When I'm on my travels, I'm no longer me but an ambassador for myself. And here are my credentials: As soon as the train set off, I let go my curiosity. I unleashed it into the compartment like a fox-terrier. My ears were alert, my eyes took in everything. I became so receptive as to be almost porous, almost permeable.

The passengers were all English. Two very elegant young women 'darlinging' each other to death. They've probably known each other for all of two days, I should think. One of the things which the English (so un-chilly themselves) find chilling in us is the ceremonious progression of formalities that takes place between fashionable women in France. The successive stages leading from '*chère madame*' to '*chérie*' do not exist over here, where all forms of preamble are despised.

These ladies were wearing skirts two centimetres lower than is chic. Though it was clear that some of the best

36

couturiers in Paris were responsible for their attire, there was a tiny hint of exaggeration which gave their Englishness away. Too much jewellery, for example; too deep a cleavage and a tiny hint of colour in hats that were meant to be worn dead black. One felt that they were suffering from being so soberly dressed. They chain-smoked (another self-indulgence) all the way from Paris to Calais.

Next to them was another English woman but this one was the old-fashioned kind. Enormous. Travelling on her own. Wearing about ten huge, battered gold bracelets that bore the baby-tooth marks of all her children and, with hair as wild as a chrysanthemum, she chased after porters, giving orders in a peremptory but nervous voice. Her sail-like veils floated behind her and, with one hand, she clutched her wreck of a hat. No one found her the least bit funny. Nor did anyone see the pathetic side of this old and stubborn bloom.

But to get back to the compartment. Two gentlemen sitting opposite two ladies. The latter can barely restrain their enthusiasm while the two men breathe order, control, steadiness and security. Their very clothes seem to have grown on them and to be as integral a part of them as bark on a tree. From time to time they bring from their pockets objects made of chased gold. They are the epitome of stylishness.

I always feel depressed when I travel with English people. In comparison to them everything seems wilted. I think I should prefer to travel with four generations of a Latin family, all decked out in dusty mourning black – like the people you can see on our trains.

As the train approaches its destination, the atmosphere becomes more and more refined. All moves on oiled wheels and the Pullman staff go about their business with such smooth and quiet efficiency you might be in one of the best hotels in the world, having hand picked your own private personnel.

37

There is no pushing and yelling; as our luggage is unloaded and, as we all get off the train, we fall under the benign influence of that sovereign of British adminstration, the policeman . . .

My carriage swings merrily through this neat, trimmed-down countryside in which every field seems to wear the particular livery of its proprietor. The great open spaces of France have disappeared. Like a low Tudor ceiling, the sky hangs over a landscape as clearly and precisely delineated as a chessboard. The tracks follow the walls of a park in which stands a red-brick manor dating from Elizabethan times and reminding me of all that I love about England. I love its restfulness, its good manners, its humour, its little grocery shops that sell everything from caviar to crêpe-soled shoes; I love its Queen Anne architecture, its birds, its ghosts. (In France we have so few birds and even fewer ghosts.) I love its country-house life, with its stiffly starched housemaids and its bath-salts. (In France we have no housemaids and frugality dictates that bath-salts are not provided for guests.)

I am amazed by the great flat-chested English ladies whose indeterminate shapes are suggested by the discreet positioning of small pieces of jewellery. A childlike innocence pervades the no-man's land of their bodies and in the distant heights of their aloofness is great shyness. For you must admit, the English are really good people at heart. They ask for nothing better than to give, to give of themselves, that is. How cordial is their handshake, their offer of a loan, how frank they are about their love-life! They shrink from nothing! Have you noticed how generously they give stories to the newspapers about their families? How they rent out their houses, just as they are, never dreaming of hiding all those compromising letters, all those signed photographs, all the fly-leaf dedications that lie within?

38

According to my mother, this kind of frankness and generosity is not typical of the Scot who looks down on his expansive English neighbour much as our northerner looks down on the Midi.

I shall have to see if she was right. Mother is the only Scot I have ever known and maybe not all her compatriots are as discreet as she was. I remember very little of Aunt Agnes, who will no doubt be playing rather an important role in my immediate future. When I was a child, she used to remind me of a dry, light russet leaf driven willy-nilly by the wind.

This is such a strange letter. No mention in it of either you or me. But then how could there be, when I am in mid-flight, as it were, and my foot is poised to step at last on *terra firma*.

Sauge to Alain

Glendrocket, Perthshire, N.B.

Here I am at last! On a completely different planet. It's hard to imagine being further away from you; all the more reason for clinging desperately to you as proof of my own existence; I'd otherwise begin to doubt I was alive. So let me float with you on the fragile raft of these letters; I shan't attempt to hide the fact that we are completely adrift on an unknown sea, but be patient and listen to the tale of your own Ancient Mariner.

In a spotless, comfortable, well sprung private compartment, my anxious frame was carried up all the way from King's Cross to Perth. As you know, I can never sleep on trains and this trip was no exception. Also, my hunter's instinct was well to the fore. Here was another country opening into my sights, so all through the rhythmic swinging of the night I *spied* on the land of Scotland. Whenever we stopped, we were immediately engulfed by silence. The cosy little stations match the diminutive trains that look like toys compared to our enormous European locomotives. Then towards dawn I dozed off and was suddenly awoken by a gust of air so fresh as to beggar description. It could have been air from the beginning of time.

I lifted up the blinds, expecting to witness some kind of miracle. My eager eyes beheld a beautiful landscape of moors separated by crumbling walls, stretching as far as the eye could see and covered with all the colours of heather from ecclesiastical violet to palest, most delicate pink. Then, set like a jewel in the heather, a small lake appeared. The gentle slopes of the mountains guard it on all sides and one could imagine its surface has never reflected a human face. The whole effect is one of softness and solemnity, like that of a young angel who never yet has loved. It seemed always to be morning here. I am still new enough to the place to 'see' it intuitively, so to speak, and to view it from a distance. Would that this state of sweet and blissful ignorance might remain! As soon as I put my foot on the ground, however, my instinctive values will be changed.

But to continue; at Perth, I was met by an ancient limousine, the interior of which, smelling as it did of camphor and mushrooms, was more like some den or grotto than a motor-car. It was driven by a blubber-lipped and taciturn young man who answered all my questions with a guttural grunt. In a very few minutes, we were clear of the hideous town with its tall, gaunt houses and their windows, so awkwardly close together they looked like children's drawings. To my surprise the hinterland beyond was utterly magical! Soon we were in a landscape full of wafery ferns, delicate scilla and dandelion clocks – a carpet of flowers worthy of an early Flemish canvas. We passed as in an aquarium, through tunnels of the darkest green, until finally the castle itself appeared, looking lonely and forbidding. It bristled with turrets, pitted all over with small, mean little windows from which at any moment one expected to see a witch's head appear.

This fortress, completely restored during the Victorian period, had been built for the purpose of defence. So what would have been the point of trying to make it beautiful? I should imagine that your ordinary fairy castles are few and far between in Scotland.

At the entrance, a little red-haired lady, dry and brittle as a biscuit, is waiting to greet me. This is my Aunt Agnes, Lady Balquidder. She darts her pointed face towards me, brushes my cheek and I am made welcome. Her brisk little voice suits her well; in a telegraphic style, she enquires about the journey, the crossing, my mother's health, etc. . . . She scurries and bustles about; how many trunks do I have? are they registered? did I have enough English money? What! haven't I had any lunch on the train? Fortunately she has thought of that. Follow me, she instructs, and as she hops jerkily on ahead, I follow this little sparrow.

Now, imagine a very long, very high-ceilinged dining-room. It was built over the site of a disused chapel and has kept the same shape. Light oak panelling covers half its height, like a corset, and portraits of ancestors line the walls between panel and ceiling. Some of these are shown wearing the plaid thrown over the shoulder. Although it is the 16th of August, the room smells of damp and feels icy.

If you thought you had any idea what a Scottish breakfast is, you would be very much mistaken. Let me enlighten you. First there is porridge, with bits of oatmeal left in on purpose, to be chewed within the mouth. Real Scots porridge should not be reduced to a mash, as is popularly believed; there should remain, somewhere deep inside it, some hard lumps that have been merely softened up, as it were. Over all this you pour a rich, golden, oleaginous cream; tradition requires that you eat it from wooden bowls and standing up. Only heathens, Agnes tells me, eat porridge sitting down.

You are then led to a kind of magician's screen behind which is set out an array of eggs and bacon, kippers and kedgeree (which is a sort of pilaff based on chopped salmon). Having been introduced to these strangers, so to speak, you are led to the large table where scones, honey and oatcakes await you. In Great Britain the real meals are breakfast and tea; lunch and dinner are extras to which no one pays very much attention.

During all this time, Aunt Agnes had been getting more and more chatty. She didn't seem to expect me to talk back so I could get on with quiet thinking on my own. However, I did interrupt her once to ask about my two young cousins.

'Are they perhaps away from Glendrocket at the moment?' I ventured politely, knowing perfectly well that they were never away from the place.

The wrinkled old face took on a furtive, almost cunning look. When she was young, she must have looked very much like a fox.

'No, they're here . . . home,' she whispered, darting a terrified glance behind, as if they might be crouching behind some screen. 'It's just that they're very shy, you know; they're not very experienced in the ways of the world . . .'

My curiosity, already at fever pitch, needed little more to plunge into the wildest conjecture. All day long, without showing, I had in fact been looking out for them, feeling their mercurial, mocking presence quite close. The young twins had indeed become legends in their own short lifetime.

As time went on, Aunt Agnes' agitation increased. Her gestures, *staccato* at the best of times, became positively epileptic. Two empty places at the lunchtable did decidedly nothing to improve the situation. She seemed to think it incumbent upon her to apologize for the way

she had brought them up. They were, she said
'impossible children'. 'In France,' she added, 'you don't
have children like that', as one might say, 'In France you
don't have bandits now, do you? You don't see wolves
any more?'

Would they make an appearance at dinner or had they
put their camping plan into operation? their victim
wondered. The dinner gong was struck. Agnes and I
were perched in two tapestry-covered armchairs at the far
end of the vast library and I was doing my best to
entertain her with stories about Paris friends dead long
before my time. Suddenly there was a commotion on the
other side of the door; the sound of hesitant steps
approaching, going away, reapproaching; there was a
good deal of whispering and shifting about. Then the
door suddenly opened and a person, obviously pushed
from behind, catapulted into the room. It was Malcolm.

Once in, he dragged his feet uncomfortably and
bumped into the furniture. My aunt's relief was obvious
from her pitiful 'Ah'. Introductions were made. He
tendered an enormous, recalcitrant paw to me as into the
dimly lit room came another figure, feeling its way
against the walls as if afraid of being pounced on. This
was his sister. Much as I was dying to, I did not look at
her. Unlike her brother, she gave me a hearty, finger-
crushing handshake. The two silent shadows went and sat
as far away from Aunt Agnes and myself as possible.

Feigning indifference, I took up the earlier conversation
with my aunt and tried to put a little animation into the
stories I knew through hearsay alone. I could tell that the
twins were listening avidly. My idle chatter fell into a
silence as deep as the jungle where animals breathe,
unseen. Fortunately, dinner was then announced. They
followed as from a distance; curious but wary by-
standers.

By happy chance, the dining-room was better-lit than
the drawing-room. Agnes had put me to sit on Malcolm's

43

right and his sister opposite me. I was now, therefore, in a position to take a good look at her.

First of all, I realized and was touched by the fact that these primitive creatures had actually dressed for dinner. What a struggle it must have been to put on that dinner jacket, only a sleeve and one slightly frayed lapel of which was visible to me. The sister, the disconcertingly named Jean, was got up in a dress that looked as if it had once been curtain-material. One wondered how, by what miracle, her magnificent shoulders were restrained from bursting out of the narrow garment's constraints; on her it seemed like some form of prison garb which she wore with dignity. She would have made a very good figurehead. Dark curls hung like bunches of grapes on either side of her cheeks, setting off a chin that was round and cleft. As for the eyes, masked also by a thick mop of hair, they were impossible to fathom. I suspected that she might be beautiful.

Dinner, remarkable only for its total lack of flavour, consisted of a clinically tasteless soup and sterilized turbot. It did nothing to revive either the guests or the conversation.

Deciding that attack was the best means of defence I said to my neighbour:

– What is the name of that very bushy kind of hill plonked in the middle of the park like a bunch of flowers on a giant's table?

– I don't know.

– Malcolm, really! Would you *kindly* answer your cousin? Aunt Agnes, a tiny bundle of energy, was furious.

– Why should he? I said, shrugging my shoulders. I'm not in the least bit interested anyway, as it happens.

I had no choice but to recognize a pact of silence on their part, and decided that since they seemed to agree with each other about everything, I should not address another single word to him. For poor Agnes, I renewed my conversational efforts. I told her all sorts of stories, mostly made up on the spur of the moment, about all her dear friends in Paris; I opened up whole photograph albums in her mind; called up as well as I could the faded glories of Bayreuth; asked her hundreds of questions about Glendrocket, about her own past, about local folklore, and so forth. I could feel the twins' hostility rising as secrets were divulged and the possibility of betrayal increased.

Then I started to ask her about the family portraits in the dining-room. As I pointed to them, she told me their names, and when we came to the portrait hanging just above Jean's head and showing a florid young man in a tartan waistcoat, Aunt Agnes said:

– And that one there is Angus MacFinnish, the children's great-grandfather. It's attributed to Raeburn, one of our greatest Scottish painters.

Suddenly lowering my finger, I pointed directly at Jean herself.

– And that one? I said. To whom is it attributed?

This little impertinence of mine was greeted with a shout of laughter. Saved! I had managed to make Jean laugh! On my left, I saw her brother's cheek flush . . . He must have given her a glare, for she now started to press her lips tight together in an effort to contain the giggle bubbling up within her. She was only a child, after all. It would have been impolitic to capitalize on this gain. I affected not to notice the breach in their defences and continued my tour of the paintings. Dinner proceeded to a close without incident. The hours following it scarcely differed from those that preceded, in that I was naturally very careful not to address the twins. Instead of disappearing, however, they were civilized enough to come and sit close to the fireplace, where I could observe them casually. All I had seen of Malcolm throughout dinner was his cheek and a bit of ear, neither of which can tell you a great deal about anyone, you must admit. Now I could savour all of him, feature by feature.

He, too, was good-looking. He had the same wild, tangled dark hair as his sister, but his features were not as fine as hers. They were regular, almost animal-like (in humans this doesn't often indicate intelligence, does it?) and his skin was dark and golden at the same time, a Dionysian skin like – ah! there it was again! The same unformulated question came into my mind as when I had seen his sister. Like an unfamiliar sound in the night that one waits to hear repeated and confirmed, the question had come up again: why so golden? why so dark also? They looked like gipsies but, from their stature, gipsies who might have married their daughters into a northern aristocracy. The physique was Scottish but the colouring Romany. When, in a low voice, I asked her, Aunt Agnes told me that the Scots could be divided into two types, dark and red, and the dark ones could often claim southern ancestry.

A thousand impressions crowded in on me and I was already looking forward to analysing them at my leisure. Claiming tiredness, I kissed my aunt, who by this time was very tired herself from all the excitement. I prepared myself for the long walk to bed, along dimly-lit corridors, up the ringing staircase, past the small, stiff, creaking doors that appeared to lead into so many cells . . . And here I am in my own room, at last. It is lit by a smoky lamp which projects onto the ceiling a pagoda-shaped shadow. And as ill-luck would have it there is a failure in the newly-installed electricity system . . .

I undress modestly, so as not to offend the sensibilities of this disapproving room, which has probably never sheltered a naked woman before. A kind of groan goes up, swells and lingers . . . I turn round and recognize a friend, the wind. Has it crept in stealthily here to find me, I wonder? Who knows, this very wind might already have passed through Vincy, bearing on its breezes the fragrance of France! I remember that this wind might also have been the friend and comforter of Marie Stuart when everyone had been banished from her sight. Greetings, dear compatriot! As these inhospitable walls glower down upon me, I shall listen to the secrets you have to tell.

CHAPTER THREE

The twins were sprawled on a shapeless, lumpy divan whose stuffing was falling out and which they called their 'parliament'. This was where all the affairs of State, that's to say, of Glendrocket, were decided. Today the twins, Jean in particular, were serious, yet excited.

– Well I'm just telling you. I don't think she's *too* bad!
– Ah, she's got you round her little finger, I can see, grumbled Malcolm, sucking on his eternal humbug.
– Not at all. But let's be fair, I mean you *were* really crude, answering her like that.
– Oh *crude*, eh? I'm crude now, am I? And I thought you said she hadn't made a conquest!
– Oh, shut up!

Jean's hands began to flail wildly as she went for her brother's hair.

– Ouch! You're hurting me!
– Don't say stupid things then!
– Stop! That's enough.

Then silence.

– Now where were we? For he, too, was dying to broach the dangerous subject.
– Well, I was just saying that if she'd wanted to, she could have really made trouble for you; but instead of

that, she simply said she wasn't interested and then she
didn't speak to you any more. So you ended up looking
like a badly-behaved little boy with no table-manners!
– Thanks! You don't mince words, do you? That's very
kind!
– Well, you know it's true.
– You're horrible. What are you trying to do? Make me
say she's lovely?
– You soon will, murmured Jean. She knew her brother
of old.

Then silence again, broken only by the sound of chewing.
The humbug was sucked enough now and ready to be
crunched. Soon a strong minty smell pervaded the
atmosphere.

– What *do* you think of her? Jean wheedled.
– Hmm . . . not as bad as I expected. What do you?
– Did you notice the colour of her eyes?
– Honestly! I didn't go over her face with a magnifying-
glass, you know!
– But you can't have failed to notice the colour of her
eyes.

Malcolm allowed himself to be drawn.

– What are they like then?
– Black. They're black, like . . .
– Don't be silly, they're blue!
– You see? You *did* notice! proclaimed his sister
triumphantly.
– And her hair? Do you remember what we thought
she'd be like? Small and swarthy?
– I suppose it's funny really, Malcolm finally
acknowledged, adding hastily: She's a damn nuisance, all
the same. Just think, we won't be able to move without
bumping into her.

Sauge to Alain

Alain, my darling heart,

I'm clinging to you more and more – oh yes I am – you represent *terra firma* and this sea I am adrift on is more than a little frightening. I can see the little pink peaks of unsuspected reefs, and strange fish swimming in its depths. Yet I am happy and I do have some secret pleasures. I'm probably hiding my contentment under a façade of disapproval so as to propitiate the gods. If they knew, they'd say: So you think you're happy. Take *that*. So when I complain, do understand it's just for appearances.

Bless you for being so French and so positively so! Everything here is murky, and vague and dim. If I don't do so already I shall soon start believing in ghosts. It's so they can walk about them more easily, I suppose, that the rooms here are so enormous. I'm trying to find out what the meaning of these great inhospitable spaces *is*. Why do they look so empty and lunar? You could even say there's something rather voracious about them. I've tried as hard as I can, but with no success, to 'colonize' my own room; I toss in the occasional couple of cushions, the odd covering, here and there; half an hour later I come back in and find they've disappeared. *The Room with the Ravenous Appetite* – it could be a new Wells novel! It is hard to imagine people crying, dancing, singing, laughing or loving in these pale, empty moons of rooms. Yet the castle is ancient and must have seen a lot in its time. Parts of it date from the fifteenth century and the whole place reminds you of dungeons and thumbscrews and gallows. For example, there is nowhere more sinister than the very turret I'm in now; the walls are redolent of the blood of its victims, and bats brush past you on the spiral staircase.

My cousins have broken their vow of silence to invite me on a tour of the place, but I smelt a rat. They are still young, and wild enough to think nothing of shutting me up in some oubliette and letting me out two or three days later, half-dead with hunger and terror. So it was old Agnes who did the honours. Along she went, in front of me, holding a candle dripping drops of wax as she proceeded . . .

I never did like the Middle Ages, though they can be forgiven a great deal for having produced Villon; his life would not have been nearly so romantic if he'd lived a century later – and that after all was the *French* Middle Ages. It had some lighter moments in the doom and gloom; the Baux's Court of Love was not far off; the Popes at Avignon were too busy collecting recipes to be bothered with papal bulls, but in Scotland, the Middle Ages were really grim . . .

There were no troubadours or fools to take the bloodthirsty lords down a peg or two; the weak Scottish sun never managed to get through the bars of their forts, and Macbeth was only one of many. How many other murdered guests were there of whom we never hear? The feudal mentality lingered in Scotland long after England was well into the Renaissance when masquerades and madrigals were all the rage.

I was anxious to return to the so-called 'seminary' part, the Victorian wing of the castle. 1860s' chandeliers hang from the ceilings there, dripping massive squares of crystal; and the inevitable white lace curtains that scratch you as you pull them only emphasize the great distance between ceiling and floor. The few dwarfed pieces of furniture give no suggestion of warmth or habitation and the only touch of gaiety comes from the carpet, a worn but very cheerful tartan. It reminds me of Bonnie Prince Charlie, as elusive as love itself, and his secret accomplice who hid him in an oak some five hundred yards from the castle.

But the minute you step outside, everything is wonderful and that's what counts, isn't it? the beauty of the earth? After being here only twenty-four hours I have come to realize that in this part of the world, domestic life is utterly without importance. You go back home only for meals; sometimes you even take sandwiches, to eat out in the fresh air. Already I've slipped into this habit, which in fact saves me from having to endure interminable luncheons alone with my Aunt Agnes (the twins return for dinner only). It's clear that she prefers to lunch off a tray, and equally clear to me that I prefer sandwiches on the banks of our little loch. This flashes like a monocle, high up on the velvet moors. In order to get there, you have to climb the hill I so unfortunately likened to a giant's bouquet the other day. The hill itself is encircled by a little babbling brook in whose waters the most ordinary object is transformed; a rusty old tin can full of holes becomes a brilliant red *bonbonnière* as well as the secret hideout of a trout. Near the single bridge that spans it there hangs a piece of leather which the waters have turned a bluish-black.

Over pebbles speckled like kestrels' eggs a shoal of small trout swim; a branch cracks, paralysing them with fear. I clap my hands and they rush, as one, to shelter in the shadows of the bridge. A family of deer lives on this hillside, Aunt Agnes tells me. So I creep steathily along, stopping to pick up a jay's feather, blue as the skin of mackerel. Further on I find a tuft of bloodstained fur, large white feathers mingled with it – testimony to some nocturnal struggle, of owls I imagine; to prey is natural in this part of the world, I would say.

And today, just imagine! I had an adventure. As I came towards the top of this hill, I heard footsteps. You know how good I am at hiding! Quickly, I climbed up a little pine-tree with branches close enough together for me to haul myself up to a decent height in next to no time. There was thick greenery in the trees and I was safely out of sight, waiting with my heart beating like mad. The footsteps approached. It was Malcolm and Jean. There

they were, walking confidently along, feeling perfectly at
home and in their element. They were just about to pass
beyond my tree when I couldn't resist it. As Jean's curly
head got within just a few yards of me, I leaned through
the branches and called out softly, 'Jean!' She gave a cry
and threw herself into her brother's arms. Their two kilts
swirled together. So there is something womanly about
Jean after all! This was the first time I had seen her do
anything feminine.

In daytime, they both dress exactly the same: white
flannel shirt, tie, little short jacket, kilt and sporran. They
cannot be told apart. Only in the evening do they become
reintegrated into their respective sexes.

All this makes me yearn to see a really womanly
woman again; the sort of smart, elegant, affected and
frivolous woman you so rightly love, my dear.

Alain to Sauge

Bagnoles-de-l'Orme,
August 22nd.

My dear child,

I hasten to reply to your disarmingly and suspiciously
long letter. You only write these screeds when you badly
need to confess your latest infatuation to some confidant,
even if it's only your husband. You'll always need me,
you know; you've often said so yourself. I'm the only one
upon whose discretion you can rely always, for the very
good reason that indiscretion would make me look
foolish.

I am wary of the effect Scotland is having on a mind
vague enough as yours already is. I don't mean to suggest
by this that it's in any way inferior; on the contrary, you
know how much I admire it. But do beware of your
imagination; it's a trick mirror that sometimes makes

things look bigger than they are, and sometimes smaller
. . . If I were to subject your castle, your twins, and your
Scotland to the scrutiny of an impartial eye (my own, of
course), I wonder what I would see.

I suspect it would turn out to be an extremely
uncomfortable, freezing old barracks of a place, inhabited
by two dull hairy country bumpkins with no
conversation whatsoever. From what you say the sister
sounds horrible. You know how much we men like tall
women. This one sounds like a giant.

As for Scotland, well . . . Obviously Scotland is not
entirely devoid of charm but it does rain all the time, the
food is appalling and you'll never convert me into eating
porridge; I know what I'm talking about despite never
having tasted it *in situ*. As for the rest . . .

No, darling, all things considered, you are much to be
pitied. You may not think so at the moment but
eventually you will. The disease must take its course; it's
at its peak now. This time last year, I well remember,
you felt the same about Hungary.

Meanwhile, life here is not too bad – despite the rigours
of the *cure*. I have plenty of time to observe what's going
on around me. Yesterday a charming young woman
arrived; Sandra Fantecchi's sister, have you met her? She's
like a very good Van Dongen.
(Let's hope this works, murmured Alain to himself. Let's
hope Sandra does have a sister. Mustn't overdo things –
just a hint of a sister should do the trick for the moment.)

No need to remind you to write, my enchanting
magician, I know I'm the little boy from the audience you
ask to come up and hold your watch for you . . .

Blessings, you wretch!

Alain

The twins were lying, sphinx-like on their 'parliament'.

54

– Well I'd never have thought it of her, said Jean
reprovingly.
– Why not? She can go wherever she likes, retorted her
brother.
– But I mean, spying on us like that!

Jean was highly indignant.

– Don't be so silly. How could she be spying on us or
springing on us if she was there first?
– I tell you she went up there on purpose!
– You're mad, my dear girl. You're so furious, you've
lost your senses. What makes you think she wants our
company? On the contrary, she seems to go to
considerable lengths to avoid us. When we go out she
nearly always chooses the opposite way from ours.
– You sound as though you mind.

Malcolm's face flushed.

– Do you really want a clout?

But this time, Jean was not to be intimidated. Leaping
nimbly off the divan, she ran to the other side of the room.

– I'm not blind, you know. When you saw her in that
tree, you couldn't move, and I wish you could have seen
the stupid, idiotic look on your face!

At this, a nicely-aimed book landed squarely in Jean's
stomach. She ignored it.

– You can't make me shut up. What about those nice
clean nails then? What about that neatly-brushed hair?
You don't think I haven't noticed, do you?
– !!!
– You big softy! I suppose some people might be taken
in, but *not me*! I've been watching it all!
– I'll get you this time! yelled Malcolm, hurling himself
in pursuit of his sister.

Like two puppies, they rolled over and over on the carpet together . . . Unusually for these days – for their games lately were not the happy tussles of before; they teased and insulted and dared each other less. Their dependence upon each other was turning into a burden. Each watched the other to see who would give in first. Through sheer boredom they were beginning now to become almost civilized.

And for the twins, being civilized meant being offered tea by the gamekeepers' wives. Since there were three game-keepers, this meant three teas; gatherings at which they silently and fatalistically gorged themselves. After their third orgy it might have seemed the twins had reached the apotheosis of gluttony, but the supreme feast was yet to come. This consisted of tea at the head gamekeeper's house. Although she had never left the lodge, Mrs Bracken, like most ordinary people in the Highlands, was intelligent and well-educated. Her graceful and easy manner would not have shamed the wife of an ambassador. Her husband, whom she inevitably referred to as 'the Master', was also carpenter to the castle. With his drooping moustaches and his narrow eyes, he looked not unlike a Samurai warrior. An honest, contempla-tive man, his only loves were the Bible, scientific books, the MacFinnish family, his dog and his wife. Both treated the family as equals, with just a touch of condescension on their part. For wasn't Lady Balquidder a 'single lady' and therefore potentially the innocent victim of any number of intrigues? As for the orphan twins, they had placed themselves squarely under the protection of Mr and Mrs Bracken since birth. Bracken himself was a kind of regent at Glendrocket. It must be remembered that their family had been established for more than a century in this part of the world and that the smaller family tree had grown in the shadow of the great one. Their lodge stood at the entrance to the park and was built like the castle itself, in the gothic style, with gargoyles and turrets jostling together for a place close to its narrow roof.

The main room was a kitchen–cum–bedroom containing

an enormous bed and a small range. On the bed was spread, like some harlequin's cast-off, an immensely shabby, multi-coloured and much-mended patchwork quilt, designed no doubt to keep rheumatism at bay. The visitor's eye then noted a whole row of saucepans hanging along one wall and looking a little like some early musical instrument. These, however, were not the most surprising objects in this bizarre chamber. The walls were covered, from floor to ceiling, with the remains of ancient, dusty and faintly remonstrative calendars. 'So many days,' they seemed to be saying. 'What have you done with so many days?' Like creditors, they reiterated, 'See? We've given you all we had', and displayed their small stubs of days, with little traces of glue still remaining.

And the sitting-room, the wonderful Bracken sitting-room 'the Master' never entered, for fear of wearing out the furniture. How can one do justice to the Bracken sitting-room? First there was its gaudy pink colour, then a mahog-any chest-of-drawers so enormous you'd think they would have had to lift the roof off to get it in; this took up part of one wall and in the middle of each of its knobs were tiny mother-of-pearl discs the young visitors at first took for glove-buttons; a grandfather-clock, whose ticking domi-nated the tiny room, stood opposite. A froth of family photographs filled and overflowed from table, mantelpiece, shelves, everything. Swarming in happy abundance, with their double frames for wings, they looked like giant moths, or a bird's-eye view of a regatta. Then there were the knick-knacks: the pack of china deerhounds sitting up heraldically; the wee lasses in tartan kilts; the porcelain lovers romantically and chastely entwined; the mantel clock flanked by Queen Victoria and the Prince Consort; the vases of pink and the candlesticks of green opaline; an entire range of the mid-nineteenth-century bric-à-brac so much sought-after by the dealers of today. Mrs Bracken's collection would now be worth many thousands of pounds.

To sit on, there were armchairs through whose chintz

loose-covers the prickly horsehair could be distinctly felt. Mrs Bracken sat bolt upright in her chair opposite. If you were wise, you asked her the things she was dying to tell you; that's to say, everything she knew about the people in the photographs.

Then, at five o'clock, she would rise and go off to prepare tea. While she was out of the room, the clock ticked the seconds away, flies buzzed and you were lulled into a deep sense of somnolent well-being . . .

But to return to the twins; they had managed to contrive an invitation to one of the delightful occasions described above and as Malcolm was cramming himself with goodies, Jean, feeling less gluttonous than usual and looking round the cluttered contents of the room, spotted a small frame half-hidden behind a group of other pictures.

– May I look at something, please? she asked Mrs
Bracken, the only person in the world to whom she was
polite.
– I say! It's Sauge! she cried.
– Mrs Bracken put on her glasses.
– That's your mother, soon after her marriage.
– Look, Malcolm, wouldn't you swear that was Sauge?
– I would indeed, he admitted, with his mouth full.
– It's very odd.
– We mean our French cousin, Jean explained, she looks
very much like our mother.
– Very much, said Mrs Bracken, unsurprised.
– Do you mean to say you know her?
– Of course I do. She passes by nearly every morning on
her walk. She never fails to stop for a bit of a chat. The
Master and I are very fond of her.

The twins were stunned. Another couple of deserters! Whom *could* one trust these days?

★ ★ ★

Sauge was having a dream. In it, she was told she would be meeting again her first love, now long-since dead. She could hardly breathe; her heart was in her mouth. Expecting only to feel the shadow of her love, she was staggered to see him in the flesh, rising from his bed, as active and vigorous as the day she had first met him. His every feature was seared on her memory. His smallest gesture stirred her heart. A movement he made from across the room felt as close as if she were next to him. And then, little by little, all faded. She seemed to understand that although a curtain was falling between them, he was flourishing like a field full of wheat, somewhere else. She awoke in deathly sadness.

Oh why wasn't Alain with her? Alain with his slightly mocking tenderness, his shoulder always ready for her to lean her weary head? How foolish she had been to leave that rock in adversity, that dispeller of all evil; his jokes and his worldly-seeming Paris banter hid infinite wisdom. Deep in his heart, there was something as traditionally valiant as a *chanson de geste*.

What was she doing in this grey desolate country? In the early light of dawn, the walls of her room seemed as high as cliffs . . . When people said 'to put someone up against a wall' this was the sort of wall they meant. Not a single crack for fingers to cling to, not a trace of colour to blur the outline of the body. It was an executioner's wall, a regicide's wall. How sharply he stands out! Every muscular contraction is noted; he is nearly as white as the wall itself. Soon they will shoot him and there will be a huge splash on its surface . . . Horrible! I won't look! Sauge was about to stop her ears so as not to hear the cries . . . How long it takes for day to come, in these northern countries. She thought of her bedroom in Paris, her bedroom at Vincy, full of safe little spots to shelter in or hide . . .

On the chest-of-drawers opposite her bed, she had arranged her collection of old glass. Bohemian glass of flawless ruby red; Venetian glass, fragile as meringues; etched German glass next to the elegant lines of the French.

The first ray of sunlight falls on them, rousing, one by one, the diamond lying dormant within each, holds it in sight, follows it for a moment, as the conductor of an orchestra holds and directs an instrument before passing on to its neighbour, and so on until the fragile ensemble bursts into a myriad conflagrations. It is the signal of awakening. Dominated by the glass, the whole room begins to shimmer. The patina of the dark furniture takes on a glow; the great Venetian mirror, blue-green in its reflection, also begins to shine. All is reflection, fluctuation and light. Sauge, thinking herself at Vincy, opened her eyes.

A single, mean beam was filtering weakly through the curtains. She realized then she would have to wait another hour before the first thin strip of light appeared on the carpet. She ran quickly to the window and drew back the curtains. It was fine; a slight mist hung still over the narrow strip of lawn which always looked like a defiant kind of parting in the thick hair of the surrounding woodland. The latter used at one time to come up as far as the entrance to the castle. The fir trees were so black and so dense as to appear almost threatening. Sauge remembered a short story she had once read as a child: *The Man Whom the Trees Loved*. In the story, as at Glendrocket, the trees grew almost into the windows; the man encouraged them, called them to him; a branch from his favourite tree, a horse-chestnut, climbed inside the room; encroaching ever further, its arms approached nearer and nearer to his bed. One morning he was found dead from strangulation . . .

Sauge shuddered. Objects seemed so much more alive than people in this weird place. Feeling the need for reassurance, she flung the window open wide. A beautiful pine-scented breeze caressed her cheeks and immediately she felt better. She had nothing to fear from the trees, from animals . . . A comforting thought from her childhood returned. As long as I am *outside*, she thought, I shall be all right. In the open air, life seemed innocent, but in rooms like these . . . And why was it, she wondered, that traditionally, only old houses were haunted? Her room in the so-called modern part of the castle, the wing dating from 1860, seemed on reflection almost more sinister than the mediaeval tower. The latter's ghosts, the conventional prisoner dragging his chain, the executioner with his axe, were tame and somehow harmless. But the more recent ghost, of the deceived husband, the disinherited nephew who died in misery, the wilful sister who was locked up in an asylum; those were the real horrors. Far more frightening than what is obviously different are the things closest to ourselves: the liar, the pervert, the sadist or the spy that each of us might have become.

Historical figures, viewed from a comfortable distance, rarely seem like real murderers and are more difficult to imagine. Sauge felt herself surrounded by waxworks figures dressed in frock-coats, wearing sidewhiskers and bearing a strong resemblance to our fathers and uncles. Sixty years ago, all criminals would have looked respectable. She was far less frightened of the ugly stereotype than the handsome contemporary rogue with the voice of an angel.

As Sauge was musing thus, there was a knock at her door. It was the chambermaid with her morning tea and two lacy slices of bread-and-butter. The timely appearance of this girl walking into the room with a rustle of starched petticoats, brisk and scrubbed to within an inch of her life, brought Sauge out of her stupor.

Everything returned to normal. Her bloodstained walls and her top-hatted ghosts, now stripped of all romance, retired modestly from the stage and the sun, growing stronger by the minute, challenged her. 'Come on! Give in! Come out!' it seemed to say, and Sauge, herself again by now, laughed at its boldness. The memory of Alain faded. He became small, very small, a small Frenchman running a little to fat, a child of a man making grand phrases.

Aunt Agnes was expecting her friend Mrs Campbell for tea. Although the latter lived quite close to Glendrocket, the

ladies only visited each other once a month so as to allow
time for news to accumulate. Had they met more frequently
the conversation might well have languished. Not so today,
however! Sauge's visit was bound to be their chief topic and
so interesting did their talk promise to be that Lady Balquidder had invited Mrs Campbell a little early. Mrs Campbell,
in turn, had thought to bring with her one of her daughters,
in order to make conversation with the young visitor and
also to 'practise her French'. The ladies arrived accordingly
at about half-past four and were received in the icy drawing-
room. As if rehearsed, Sauge was not yet back from her
walk.

Mrs Campbell seemed to be descended from a race apart.
She was a giant of a creature, vaguely human but by no
means womanly; her features were tiny, and her gestures
also disproportionately small. It was surprising to see in this
extraordinary face the same shapes and configurations as in
others. The nose, for example, was recognizably a nose and
the mouth a mouth, but the curious thing was that they were
so much less sharply defined than normal; the mouth was a
mere button, the nose a kind of fold; the flat, tiny ear was
like a pheasant's and her character too was timid, bashful and
unformed. Her appearance and demeanour were therefore as
terrifying as if a mountain had not simply moved but
positively minced, or as if a tall bell-tower had suddenly
blushed. She loved clothes, perfume, gossip and intrigue.

Her eldest daughter Peggy, slightly more human than her
mother, was still a mere sketch of a girl, and though
extremely well-educated, she too was very timid. Peggy
considered social visits the worst kind of torture. Old Lady
Balquidder was all right, but at the thought of having to
meet a total stranger and be obliged, no doubt, to compli-
ment her on her English, Peggy was filled with horror.

Meanwhile her mother was speaking to Lady Balquidder:

– I have managed to persuade Neil to come and pick me
up.

Neil was her husband.

– 'cellent, replied Lady Balquidder who, in her haste to
finish speaking, never spoke whole words.
– He's dying to meet the little French girl, Mrs Campbell
crowed.

This in fact was not true; what her husband had said was:
'If you absolutely insist on my coming, do remember this
will be the last time I shall get involved. Understood? Good!'
Peggy, sitting on the edge of her chair and listening to the
conversation, kept one eye on the door. God! how ugly
Glendrocket is, she thought to herself, and how much nicer
was their own home with its small, cosy furniture, its family
squabbles and its friendly old smell of pipe-tobacco. She felt
as uncomfortable as at the dentist's; come to think of it, this
lugubrious place wasn't at all unlike a waiting-room . . . oh
to run away before it was her turn to perform. With nothing
better to do, she went through her thoughts again. They had
already been examined minutely; and were as old as the
magazines on the tables at home; that sweater had holes in
the elbows, she must get a new one; and shoes . . .
Her elders were sitting squeezed on the narrow sofa from
which she caught snatches of their conversation:

– Malcolm . . . Jean . . . impossible children . . . Sauge's
influence . . .

Those wild things? thought Peggy. They must have given
her a wonderful welcome! Presently the door opened and a
young, red-haired woman approached. After the usual introductions, she came automatically to sit next to Peggy. The
latter's heart began to beat wildly. Would she manage to find
something to talk about? But the visitor took charge.

– How I love your country, she said. I knew before
coming that it would be marvellous, but I didn't expect
to be quite so bowled over.

It was obvious she meant what she said and her English was flawless. Relieved, Peggy made so bold as to look up at her. To begin with, all she noticed was the hair, the wild red hair that seemed to flicker in small flames above the serene brow and the calm and beautiful face. She has Scottish hair, thought Peggy. Then the eyes; they were a particularly pure blue . . . no doubt she possessed a nose and a mouth but these were secondary features, vassals to the first. Peggy, who had no clothes sense, nevertheless knew that the visitor was dressed impeccably and that great care had been taken over her appearance. She knew that she was more womanly than the others; that she carried within her something ancient and immutable. Like Circe, she was powerful but possibly unaware of it . . . Peggy was shocked by the boldness of her own thoughts – it was as if someone was whispering them to her. What did she know about Mme de Cervallon? Nothing, less than nothing. Yet involuntarily, thoughts about her kept rising like messages from spirits . . . This woman is not wicked, she is simply unaware, they whispered, this morning she may do a little smuggling, tonight she will drink with the excise-men; her conscience will be clear for she will, quite simply, have forgotten. Peggy's brothers used to tease her about her intuition – was she wrong in this instance? Lost in thought, she blushed to hear Mme Cervallon gently repeat a question a second time:

– And do you live in the country all the year round?
– Oh no, not all year. We spend the winter in Edinburgh.
– How I should love to get to know Edinburgh!
Edinburgh people are so nice, or so I've always been told.
Isn't it true that the leaders of society there are excellent ladies who hold 'salons' to which they are as devoted as were the habituées of Mme de Staël?
– That's very true, concurred Peggy, forgetting her shyness. I know one or two Gibbonses but the Benjamin Constants are a little rarer.

64

Sauge hid her surprise. What! This stiff little provincial was sufficiently interested in French writers to be able to joke about their côteries? She looked at Peggy with renewed interest.

What she saw was a large, shapeless girl, prone to blushing and awkward of gesture. Yet her masculine-looking hands were fine and sensitive, more like those of a young man than a woman's. In this strange place, thought Sauge, women rarely look like women; they're all half-boy, half-girl. As they continued to chat about Mme de Staël, Sauge resumed her inspection. Peggy's eyes, small and sparkling, made her think of the tiny stars of her own country. The thin face, pinched between two hanks of hair, was as narrow as a ravine. There is nothing *round* about her, Sauge concluded, except her voice. Peggy's voice was indeed so taking that one forgot everything else. Sauge discovered that her speech was as careful as her appearance was not. Each syllable, each consonant was as clear as a jewel placed on a velvet cushion. One of the things which had struck Sauge most, in fact, was the deliberate diction of the Scots, so pleasing in contrast with the babble of the English who murder or maim every word.

Peggy and Sauge soon discovered they had dozens of interests in common: a love of books, of music and of nature. Peggy had by now lost all her timidity and began to tell Sauge all she was longing to hear about Glendrocket, about its local history, the local flora and fauna, everything in fact that she would have liked to ask the unapproachable twins.

Peggy was a good raconteuse and had a lively sense of humour. Her rather dry anecdotes were enlivened by a sharp eye for detail and had a particular charm of their own. How could Sauge have thought for a moment that Peggy might be dull? Everything about her was quite simply charming, from her delightful mixing of fantasy with logic, her eyes, both mischievous and sympathetic, to her rebellious young prelate's hands.

– Do you know my cousins? Sauge asked and receiving a nod from the other, continued, What are they like?
– They're very good-looking, said Peggy with typical Scots reticence.
– Yes they are, aren't they? Can you imagine? Ever since I've been here, all we've exchanged is the odd monosyllable.

On hearing this, Peggy amplified:

– I'm not surprised. There was a time when my aunt and your mother maintained a pretence of neighbourly relations; they had to abandon it in the end since your cousins were a real danger at the time. They used to resort to the most feudal measures to get rid of unwelcome visitors. I remember once, coming along the turret walk, I came to blows with Malcolm. He was about to try and hurl me off the battlements. Luckily he was a good deal younger than I was and therefore smaller. But it's Jean who's the real power; she's more intelligent than he is. She leads and he follows blindly.
– And yet my aunt says all they do is quarrel with each other!
– Don't you believe it. They adore each other underneath. If necessary they would join forces to repel any intruder.
– I'm the intruder in this case.
– So'll they'll stay away from you. As if by common accord. Unless one day you are so unfortunate as to find favour in their eyes. In which case they would tear you in half!
– Thank you very much! There doesn't seem to be much likelihood of that at the moment.

Peggy put on a mysterious look.

– More than you think.

At this moment, the door was opened. Sauge, influenced despite herself by Peggy's last sybilline utterance, rather expected the terrible twins to rush in. Apprehension turned to relief as she saw the figure of a small, hunched, shabbily-dressed gentleman approach. As he drew nearer to the group at the fireside he reminded her increasingly of Louis XI.

– Good heavens, it's Daddy! cried Peggy. Who would ever have thought he'd come!

Noisy cries and giraffe-like undulations showed that her mother was pleased.

– Neil! It's you! I knew you'd keep your word. He couldn't resist coming to see the pretty little French girl!

(For this poor woman, everything pretty had to be little.)

– Come and be introduced. Madame de Cervallon, my husband. He's a funny old chap but he can be very nice if he chooses, can't you, my poppet?

Then, turning to Sauge, she said: 'He's deaf, you know,' and gave him a playful tap that sent him staggering back.

He sat down, blinking little eyes that looked in his lined old face like shards of ice at the bottom of a rut.

He looks a little like Erasmus, thought Sauge. Yes, the Holbein portrait, thoughtful and canny. There was obviously a strong bond between father and daughter, witnessed by the grimace they had exchanged when he came in. Mr Campbell's old-fashioned clothes smelt slightly of mothballs. His little eyes now looked Sauge up and down, half approving, half mischievous.

– Well, young lady, he said in the croaky, unused and slightly distant voice of the deaf, and how do you like this damned country of ours, eh?

– Neil! protested Mrs Campbell.

Even had he heard that, it is unlikely her husband would have taken any notice.

– And don't tell me it isn't damned. It is. For several reasons: first of all because it rains here all the year round;

second because we have the finest meat and the finest vegetables produced on this earth and nobody knows what to do with them; thirdly, because we've got the prettiest women in the world and nobody knows what to do with them either; fourthly . . .

Here he stopped, for Sauge had broken into an amused smile.

– You may laugh but I assure you I'm not joking. You wouldn't laugh if you lived up here in Scotland. I'd say wonderful things about Scotland, too, if I lived in France!
– Oh *Father*, interrupted Peggy, raising her voice a little. You know you'd be furious if some foreigner were ill-advised enough to criticize Scotland.
– Of course I would! Just as I take it as my god-given right to declare that my daughter's nose is a disaster, that her hair is ghastly and she's got dreadful feet. But if anyone else were to even suggest that she was not fascinating femininity incarnate, I'd pulverize 'em.

Now Sauge understood what she was witnessing. This was the idyllic British family, revelling in chaff. In Britain, wherever you find two or three people who insult each other morning, noon and night, there, you may be sure, is perfect domestic harmony. The Mountain adored Erasmus and Peggy adored them both. Later, Sauge discovered that two other sisters and three other brothers were part of this very harmonious whole. They parted with promises to see each other again soon and, when they had left, Sauge began to talk about the visitors to Lady Balquidder. After her customary three-sniff preface, she replied:

– Yes, yes indeed. Very nice. Very intelligent. Very hard-working, you know. Very middle-class.

The sudden contempt which she injected into these last words discountenanced her niece. For was not Mrs Campbell this reptile's best, her only friend? She was loath, however, to challenge such a declaration and preferred to think about it all a little later.

The setting sun was casting a golden nimbus over the normally icy drawing-room. Enlivened for once by company, and bathed in this warm aura, it was almost pleasant. The smell of tea and strawberry jam lingered in the air as Sauge rose and said:

– I think I'll just go up the hillside to watch the sunset.

Now on the ground floor, under the vaulted arch of the main entrance to the castle, was a low door leading into the gunroom. This was where everything connected with sport was kept. Well-oiled guns stood in serried ranks in glass-fronted cupboards lined with green baize. Over the door hung a panoply of halberds and bills, daggers and harque-buses, shining so brightly they might have been in daily use. Sauge was later to remark that all there was in this house were engines of destruction.

On the walls were cupboards containing small stuffed beasts emerging from highly unrealistic undergrowth. Propped in a corner was a fine lacquered Harvey's fishing-rod, its slim lines contributing the only note of femininity to this masculine cavern. Behind the barred windows of the room they called the 'arsenal' the twins watched their visitors arrive and leave. Just as Sauge was stepping under the vaulted arch to walk outside, they hurled themselves upon her.

– Well, they've gone *at last*, have they? asked Jean on one side.
– We thought they'd moved in, complained Malcolm, on the other.

Sauge suddenly realized that they were furious that the Campbells had called.

– I thought they were charming, she said, annoying them even further.

Malcolm looked grave. It was worse than he thought.

69

– Really, you cannot be allowed to associate with those people.

His tone was paternal. Sauge was dying to laugh.

– Why? Aren't they . . . respectable?
– That's not the point. We are *at war* with them. We haven't spoken to each other for years.

So, there were hostilities between the clan MacFinnish and the clan Campbell. No stern father warning his daughter against the evil wiles of men could have looked more serious.

– Now you'd better understand this, Malcolm continued: Whether you like it or not, you are a member of this family and . . .
– But you seem to forget, this has nothing to do with me, interrupted Sauge, whose amusement now knew no bounds. It's not I who invited them.
– We know that. That's why we're not holding you responsible. But we thought it would be useful to let you know exactly what the situation is, said Malcolm loftily.

An icy draught whistled through the archway. Without being asked, Sauge entered the 'arsenal' and perched on a table littered with evil-smelling empty cartridges. Jean took up a position opposite her. Her feminine curiosity had got the better of her.

– I can't understand, she said ruminatively, how it is you find them charming.

And then, practically spitting the words, she added:

– They're horrible, ugly, common, dull! They can't ride; they can't shoot and they don't even know how to handle a fishing-rod!
– That's not all, sneered Malcolm. It was their filthy gamekeeper they got to shoot, *shoot*, mind you, my dog just because of worrying their damn sheep!

– It's bad enough that Aunt Agnes should invite them here, without involving you, reprimanded Jean.

Neither twin seemed to have noticed having slipped from total silence into familiarity. A strange excitement gleamed in Sauge's eyes.

– I can see whoever I like. Sometimes a person needs kindred spirits to talk to.

The twins looked at each other and Malcolm, on the point of lighting his pipe, stopped in mid-gesture. Then Jean, in a strangled voice, said:

– There's always us, you know.

CHAPTER FOUR

My dear old Alain,

Yes, you're right. I have been very lazy about writing lately. But I've been spending all my time fishing and shooting, and unless I take a pen and pad with me . . . well, you know how it is! I don't know how to convey to you the *beauty* of my situation here now!

I have been accepted by the twins! And not just accepted but finally welcomed with open arms, if you please! You may laugh (in fact I can hear you laughing all the way from France and I could shake you; I could hit you, you old Parisian, you don't know anything!). In the whole of Paris there is not a single *salon*, not one, so exclusive and so difficult to get into as the MacFinnish gunroom. And I was there! Let me tell you how the miracle occurred.

First of all, I should say that for a long time now the twins have been leading up to some kind of *détente*. They were getting a little bored with being on their own but would not for the world admit defeat. At the exact psychological moment, fate introduced into the proceedings a nice neighbouring family who had somehow transgressed (something to do with livestock) and incurred their wrath. Aunt Agnes having committed the unpardonable sin of inviting these disgraceful characters for tea, the twins, in order to prevent my being converted to the side of the enemy, decided to enter into negotiations with me; especially since they could now do so without sacrificing one iota of their precious pride. Anyway, the historic conversation took place in a most appropriate spot, nicknamed the 'arsenal' and bristling with pistols and cutlasses. They were so young and so serious about it that I'm afraid I was touched.

Ever since then (this was a week ago) my life has been transformed. They follow me everywhere and now instead of two pirates roaming around the place there are three of us! We fish salmon and trout. We shoot grouse and rabbit and it's lovely to see the two of them coming home laden with dead game, like sacrifice to offer the gods.

Aunt Agnes is in seventh heaven about this development and speaks even faster than usual. In the morning, if it's fine, she appears, like a lizard, on the terrace. Yesterday, at breakfast-time, she was there and, seeing me come in flanked by my two great giants, she said with a loud sniff: '. . .'zactly like Freia with Fafner and Fasolt.' For her, no circumstances in life are without Wagnerian over-tones.

In the evenings now, instead of sitting alone with Aunt Agnes, we all sit together round the fire and I try to make the twins laugh. I must say this is none too difficult, provided my story includes some gory incident or some mimicry. They don't understand pathos and, like all children, they love travel tales. It's a good thing my audience does not possess a highly developed critical sense because I say anything that comes into my head, I'm enchanted by their artlessness. They are as unconscious of the pleasure they give as the scenery you glimpse through a train window. In Jean, for example; there is a strange harmony between the face and the body. Her movements say as much as her facial expression. She frowns and smiles with her arms and legs. You feel that if she were decapitated, nothing essential would be lost. She stoops to pick something up and a swift kind of beauty shoots through her body like an arrow. You never grow tired of watching her and doing so is just like gambling. Sometimes your luck is in, sometimes not. Nothing can be more beautiful and more ugly than she can be. Now you see her, now you don't. The glimpses you can catch of her are more exciting than many an hour of studied contemplation.

The other night, I was wearing my silver lamé dress. Malcolm's face lit up like a child's when he saw it. 'Oh, can I touch?' he said ecstatically. I let him feel a fold of the cloth, and as he did so I felt like a white man about to cheat a black. Ah well, what can you do about that I wonder? There'll always be whites taking advantage of blacks, won't there? Will you forgive me?

Sauge.

Letter (not posted) from Alain to Sauge

Dearest, too dear darling,

I am appalled by what I read in your letter! I can see you only too well in your silver lamé, annihilating that poor innocent! For heaven's sake, leave those poor creatures alone! It will be terrible if you don't. You know I'm not superstitious, but I have this feeling that something very peculiar is happening and that you will be the one to suffer. I don't for a minute believe you are aware of it. I know you'd never do anything malicious on purpose. From time to time you have flashes of lucidity like when you felt guilty for letting yourself be pawed by that perfect stranger of a boy whose innocence, I might add, was threatened the minute he set eyes upon you.

Darling, please, *please*, leave those people. I beg of you,

leave them before it's too late. Of course I know I have
only to ask you to come back for you to decide to remain
for ever. What is to be done? I'm so terribly worried.

Letter (posted) from Alain to Sauge

Paris

My dear little Sauge,

I'm glad you reminded me it was six days [crossed out]
some time since I had had word of you. Life has been so
hectic lately that I'm afraid I hadn't noticed. See how
easily you might have slipped away out of the dangerous
(soapy) waters of domesticity?
     I'm delighted to hear you still have not tired of your
bumpkins. Take your time, do, coming home. I'm taken
up a lot these days both with business and the old social
round you hate so much. So I wouldn't be able to spend
as much time as I should like with you. The work on
your bedroom is coming along splendidly. We must
always keep on the move, mustn't we. Shifting our
possessions as well as ourselves. To be still is death and I
think the reason why painters put birds in their landscapes
is so as to suggest escape, evasion, liberty.
     Coming from me, these little reflections may surprise
you, but the fact is, I am contemplating a trip – yes a trip –
to each his own! A group of friends including the
Viroflays, the Villarets and the Fantecchis have asked me
to go with them on a visit to Indo-China. They leave on
November 15th and since I knew that you, of all people,
would understand this *Wanderlust*, I've let myself be
persuaded. So it's all fixed. I'm sure that having criticized
my sedentary habits for so long, you'll be delighted.
     In the meantime it's nice to be back. Paris gossip is the
best in the world. Without you, the apartment is very
dull, so I'm hoping to throw a few little dinner parties.

75

Meanwhile, I shall dine out. Will write longer in a few days.

Your sprightly,

Alain

Sauge perused the letter several times. It was not calculated to please. Alain's indifference, always lurking beneath the surface, she believed, was now obvious. She was losing him. It was a distinctly nasty thought. As for this Indo-China trip, it was simply a pretext for being with Sandra Fantecchi's sister. Her name had been slipped innocently into the party. Always if you're going to mention a suspicious name, you make sure you throw in a few others, for safety. That of Yolande de Viroflay was beyond reproach. Re-reading Alain's earlier letter, in which he first mentioned this sister of Sandra's, Sauge remembered having had a fleeting but definite premonition of something at the time. Then, obviously, he had had nothing to hide, and could talk about her openly. Now, however, her presence had to be concealed under layers of innocent-sounding names. A flash of anger zigzagged through her lowering spirits. So! He had become the life and soul of the party, had he? The great traveller was parading around the world with an Italian girl young enough to be his daughter! On reflection, she remembered that Sandra did have a ravishing younger sister in which case there was only one thing to do: return, catch Alain by surprise, take a firm grip of him and show him how inept this young girl probably was. If she was anything like Sandra, it would be an easy thing to do. She would be no match for Sauge.

It is often the case that highly intelligent people are more naive than those with mediocre minds. Their brains, tired of all the mental contortions of which they are capable, become easily confused and they fall into the most obvious traps. Simple strategies are so far outside their normal frame of reference that they are more devastated by them than by a subtle ploy. This was certainly true of Sauge. Consequently, whenever any conjugal crisis occurred, Alain found the more childish the methods he used, the more likely they were to succeed.

Quickly! thought Sauge. What was needed was a wire announcing her imminent return; a sharp whistle piercing the silence that had grown between them. Ah but the twins! she thought, not without annoyance. She had completely forgotten her rendezvous with them at six o'clock in the 'arsenal'. She may as well get it over with. She would draft the telegram afterwards. Stuffing the form in her bag, she went down.

Under the arch stood Malcolm, already waiting for her.

— Come quickly! he shouted joyfully. We've shot two
wild duck for you!
— Look, aren't they beautiful? said Jean, brandishing their
prey.
— They're for your dinner, said Malcolm, for ever
practical.
— What, both for me? said Sauge, laughing.
— They're a present, Malcolm explained, unabashed. I
shot one first and, of course, Jean was furious. Then
luckily, she shot one herself so that means we've got one
each to offer you.

'. . . And of course Jean was furious.' So they had to be equal in all things did they? How long, Sauge wondered, would this sort of competition last? Some day it was bound to happen that Jean would be beaten by her brother. Beaming now with satisfaction, they both looked at her. Sauge suddenly realized how painful her news would be to them.

— I'm afraid I have some bad news for you . . . I've got to
go, she stammered, lowered her eyes.

At first they seemed not to understand.

— Go? Go where? Now?
— Go away from here. Back to France. My husband is
asking for me . . .

An almost imperceptible 'ah' came from them, as if a brutal hand had suddenly stopped their breath.

What? I only meant to wound, not to kill, was Sauge's curious thought. For they looked devastated. Youthful and radiant a moment ago, their faces now were haggard and their arms hung pitifully by their sides. Sauge, till now transfixed, made a movement towards them in their distress.

– But . . . you mean, you will be going one day, they
said, like prisoners hearing the sentence of death, yet
heedless of its date.
– Yes! No! I don't know.

Her exhausted and shaking voice told them that all was not lost. In one bound they were at her side, alternately threatening and begging:

– No, no, we won't let you leave! We'll lock you up!
What would we do without you? You mustn't leave us!
Say you won't leave. Sauge, darling Sauge, we'll kill you
rather than let you go!

They had each taken hold of her arms. She felt their breath, with its slightly sharp, animal smell, on her neck. Damp curls clung to their sweaty foreheads. Faced with the onslaught of their combined emotion, she felt herself faltering.

– All right. You win. I'll stay a little longer.
– How long?
– Another fortnight.

Then, quite suddenly and out of genuine fright, Sauge burst into tears.

Letter (not sent) from Sauge to Alain

My darling,

I'm so terribly sad I could die. I love you and I want to

leave this place, but I can't. It's like in a nightmare when you can't move. Something is holding me back. It's paralysing me. It stops me crying out. I daren't examine my own feelings any more . . . I don't want to know . . .

Oh, if only you had the intuition to come and fetch me without being asked! I should let myself be led away with such a feeling of deliverance. I don't have enough strength any more to leave of my own volition. I've already tried. The date I planned to leave is long since past. Everything is against it. I keep coming up against obstacles that frighten me because they're not like anything I recognize. When I try to look at them closely, they slip away, mockingly.

And as for trying to go against the twins, I gave that up long ago. One cannot struggle with a force of nature. They're enormous and stupid and indomitable. What was Lohengrin like when he married, I ask myself and what will the twins be like when they cease to be gods to each other? Pity me. I'm longing to turn the next page in the story of their lives, but I feel it could well be the last.

Lady Balquidder was writing to her sister, the Marquise de Bréouge. It was a difficult letter. Sauge's visit had been an unhoped-for success: the twins were now clean and considerate and yet . . .

Along the corridors of her mind, guilty feelings began to creep stealthily. Feelings so vague and of which she was so unsure that they slid into her thoughts almost apologetically . . . At night, she dreamed of her sister, again very vaguely. In what way had Lady Balquidder failed in her duty? To what unsuspected danger had she exposed her nephew and niece? She called to mind their new unwonted punctiliousness, the awkward gestures of children trying to please . . . but to please whom? Why, Sauge of course . . . it was only natural. It was only natural that they should be dazzled by this beautiful, understanding cousin of theirs who had entered so whole-heartedly into their lives.

'Sauge is an acolyte serving all religions with equal fervour.' This was one of Alain's favourite sayings, which he loved to quote whenever his wife was drawn into some new obsession. It had happened so many times before that he had come to learn more and more about her from past experience. Lady Balquidder, however, could see, as it were, only one fold of the delightful fan that made up the character of her niece. She assumed, with no evidence to the contrary, that when the whole fan was spread, similar patterns would emerge. To Lady Balquidder's thinking, Sauge had behaved impeccably. If the twins had fallen for her, hook, line and sinker, it was hardly her fault . . . They should have remembered that Sauge was only there temporarily, and that her real life was elsewhere.

When she left, as undoubtedly she would, they would of course be inconsolable and *then* what would she do? Should she in the meantime put Sauge on her guard against the ever-increasing claims they would make upon her? They could so easily forget that she had a husband and obligations . . . Malcolm especially. Last night, Malcolm's voice, his tone were . . . Lady Balquidder was decidedly ill-at-ease. She had forgotten that voice . . . Soon, she began to feel tired and dispirited. She was too old to go into such things again. Ten years ago she would have tried to struggle, tried to think of some connection, something she could do, but now she was too old. Only a very small part of her continued to live in the present. She toyed with some of the dear, familiar things which had always lain on her desk: her seal, bearing the Balquidder arms; the red sealing-wax; the quantities of rubber bands of various sizes. It was a source of deep satisfaction to her to have such a well-stocked desk, such an island of orderliness in this dilapidated old shell of a house. She sighed, thinking now of the house she had lived in on the outskirts of Edinburgh when she was first married. It was a large, light straightforward house, untinged by any hint of mystery or lingering malice. Its spacious drawing-room was immediately welcoming, unlike here, where all the rooms seemed to conspire against her; designed to confuse her totally; not to mention the dust that gathered everywhere, and the cobwebs, and the draughts . . .

The little old lady shivered, her pen still poised above the page. Now how should she end this letter to Margaret? She drifted off again into the hidden byways of her unconscious. Dear Margaret! how lucky she was to be able to live in that beautiful house in town, snug against draughts, with its nice solid doors and its soft carpets . . . Ah Paris! In her mind's eye, she conjured up again her own old bedroom in the Rue du Faubourg Saint-Honoré. There was the *toile-de-Jouy*, there, her Beauvais tapestry-covered *bergère* with its carved wooden cupids palely embracing. A resinous fire crackled in the hearth and the shining orbs of the firedogs reflected in miniature a scene as neat and clean as a Dutch interior. Impressive family portraits adorned the walls. The mother of Armand de Bréouge, with her rings and her memories, stared romantically into the depths of the fire. Madame de la Follolie, her sprightly-looking great-grandmother, looked on, smiling ironically, and fingering in her nervous hands a piece of yellowing lace. Legend has it that Leotard was not indifferent to her charms. Only those whom we have known living seem genuinely dead; the others are all part of the sweet stuff of history. Dignified by their biographers, and with distance to lend enchantment to their characters, they vie in importance with the living. Madame de la Follolie, for example . . .

Here, poor Agnes allowed herself to subside into the welcoming past as if into a comfortable and familiar old armchair. She gave up all attempts to unburden herself and ended her letter with the usual: 'The children are well and join me in sending you much love.'

Although Mrs Campbell had never been required to swear an oath of allegiance to the family, it was generally understood that she would never do anything to harm their interests. And look at her now! Flying in the face of Campbell tradition, casting all pride and dignity aside and attempting a *rapprochement* with the enemy! And as if that were not all! Just as Mrs Campbell's neutrality could till now have been counted upon, so had the old enmity of the twins. No more! Oh what a bitter cup was life, to be sure! Not even the quaintness of the hitherto unbending twins remained. This visitor (whom Peggy says is nice, but who knows?), invited by Mrs Campbell, had accepted not only for herself but for her cousins also. It was all very well pointing out, as if in mitigation, that their mother had written not to the twins but to Mme de Cervallon. What did it matter how it had happened if the result was this? Today, at five o'clock, would see the arrival at Campbell's Den of Mme de Cervallon with the ridiculous twins in tow. Really, it was too funny. To think they once thought of them as proud, incorrigible savages. How the mighty were fallen!

Long before five, the implacable Campbells were lined up on the lawn in front of their house, ready to greet their visitors. As a family they were highly intelligent, a little disorganized, but full of humour. They also possessed the same laugh; a high whinnying, way above the human register, which acted as a kind of rallying-cry to the clan. They waited together till five-thirty. What could have happened? Had the twins, realizing the full extent of their degradation, suddenly run away at the last minute?

Not by any means! Young Alan, their look-out, came running back towards the house.

– They're coming, they're coming, he yelled, red-faced
and out of breath.

Three figures appeared at the bend in the drive. Two were large and (even from this distance) unkempt, and one of average height.

– How they've grown, murmured Peggy, who had not
seen them for years. Then, as they approached: There's
no getting away from it. They are magnificent!

It was true. Mrs Campbell's triumph in getting them to come was considerable, but on the question of attire, no compromise had been made. With their two kilts swinging together, they strode nobly forward, bareheaded and with the breeze lifting their dark, tight, blackberry-like curls. Sauge, in contrast, seemed to have been made out of finer, though less god-like, stuff. Only at the tea-table was the position reversed, Peggy thought. The more at ease and charming Sauge was, the more gauche and ungainly the twins, who seemed not to know what to do with their arms and legs. They should only be viewed outdoors, thought Peggy, casting an anxious glance to see how her own brothers were behaving. Clumsy, like the twins, but lacking their handsomeness, they were outdoing each other in trying to forget the vendetta. Peggy realized that the reason for this *volte-face* on their part was Sauge. But what about the twins? Why the devil had they accepted, Peggy wondered for the tenth time. Had Lady Balquidder perhaps had recourse to some unprecedented form of threat – confiscation of their guns? Their dogs? Something of the kind must have happened, she thought, till suddenly, in an instant, she understood. They were just finishing tea when Sauge took out her cigarette-case. Before she had time to ask for a light, Malcolm, knocking into guests and table alike, leapt forward, match in hand.

It all became clear. It was so as not to miss being in Sauge's company that they had consented to honour the gathering with their presence.

When had this conquest occurred? Once again, Peggy tried to guess Sauge's secret. Was it through coquetry that she had won the twins over? A woman like her could hardly fail to be a little flirtatious. Was it through curiosity or . . . was Sauge herself attracted by their youth and beauty? Vanity, curiosity, and power were the key factors in this mysterious conversion. Poor twins, what an inexperienced heart was theirs. *Theirs?* Why did she always think of them together? After all, Jean was a woman; surely she was not as exposed to the danger as her brother? One had grown too used to thinking of them jointly – it made one feel uncomfortable. In the end, these two exceptionally beautiful creatures, reflecting each other's beauty, as it were, became as repulsive as any other freak of nature, like the bearded lady or the man with six fingers. Once you start thinking of three or four absolutely identical people and then you continue reproducing them mentally *ad infinitum*, the whole business of population becomes a mad nightmare. It was Sauge's voice that interrupted this unpleasant thought:

– And what have I done, pray? You've hardly said hello.
Am I in your black books?

Less than an hour ago, Peggy would have found such an intimate greeting flattering. But now, the direct, self-confident way Sauge burst into her thoughts displeased her. We must remember the reticence of the Scots, and their respect for neutral silence.

– You're not, she said. I was just thinking, that's all.
– And may we know what about?
– Very ordinary thoughts.
– Give me an example, then I can see . . . Yes, later, she
said thus dismissing with a smile a fiery red-haired
Campbell who was asking her for a game of tennis. Your
sister and I have things we want to talk about.

All around them, the remains of tea lay like an abandoned encampment. Mrs Campbell, delighted with this happy turn of events, had taken the twins off to look at the garden. Jean was not very chatty, to be sure, she thought, but Malcolm, taken in hand and smartened up a little, would do very nicely for Jennifer, her youngest . . . For was he not a clan chief, a great landowner? Besides, a very large fortune must have been steadily accumulating for him since the death of his father! . . .

84

– I was thinking, Peggy took up again in a languorous voice, . . . it's a pity the twins have been . . . how shall I put it? Tamed?

– How can you say that? They didn't even bother to wash their hands before coming, cried the other.

– I don't mean physically. I mean mentally. You can see it straight away.

Sauge's expressive face became sad and, instead of the protestations Peggy was expecting, she said simply:

– Yes, I know.

Peggy began to like her again.

– But, I mean, how did it come about? The last time we spoke, you said they hardly spoke to you.

Sauge struggled for a moment with the temptation of telling this wise and perceptive person everything. She was sure, however, that Peggy would encourage her to leave and said merely:

– Well they must have decided I wasn't as silly as they thought.

Peggy did not press the point. She was the first to respect another's need for privacy. Besides, she had made her own interpretation of the events and needed no further information from Sauge. In her most impersonal voice, she said:

– Well, they're so young. They have a lot to learn still.

Sauge was careful to let the matter rest there. She regretted having come, flaunting her prizes, so to speak. You don't bring your matching ornaments out to tea; you leave them at home on the mantelpiece. She knew that Peggy had guessed correctly. She also knew that Peggy knew she knew! Sauge suddenly felt as if she were in a room full of mirrors, one on top of the other, all reflecting the same single image. It was the same fright that Peggy had experienced, imagining a population of clones earlier on. With effort, she wrenched herself away from this train of thought. Peggy was absolutely right, there was no question.

– Yes, Sauge said, almost joyfully. You're right, they are children. Silly to pay too much attention; they go to extremes.

Peggy hesitated for a moment. She hated drama but she would like to have uttered some kind of warning. Like a coward, however, she took refuge in her sense of humour, which shifted everything into a different perspective and stopped her taking people seriously.

Not enough has been written about the British sense of humour. It has an anaesthetic effect on sensitivity and allows jokes others would consider in deplorable taste to be made at the most tragic moments. It enables the English to face the worst catastrophes with a smile. For Peggy it allowed her to move from the prompter's box near the action to the comfortable heights of the gods. Cravenly donning rose-tinted glasses, she was glad to escape from the Dostoevskyan complications of other people's lives. Obviously it was a pity to see those primitives civilized, for they had become a much-loved local legend, but, when you thought of it, it was also quite funny. The image of Malcolm in top hat, leaving his card, was rich indeed, and Peggy was a keen observer of the foibles of human nature.

– Would you like me to show you the house? she said, after a moment.

Sauge accepted with a feeling of defeat. She knew that the subject of the twins would never be referred to again. Resignedly she lit a cigarette.

The Campbells' house, half farm, half manor, was charming. For the first time since coming to Scotland, Sauge felt at home. Not that the place was luxurious, or even very comfortable, but the small, low furnishings invited intimacy and the objects upon them, though not of tremendous value, were personal and powerfully evocative. The carpet had the date 1837 and their grandfather's initials woven into its meandering pattern. A little hand-drawn map of Oceania by Stevenson served as a reminder both of history and of the globe's expanses. The austerity of Scotland showed in the old granite fireplace whose mantel might have made a perch for the great golden eagles of her peaks.

The tables were strewn with books; Carlyle jostled with Aldous Huxley; Burns was back-to-back with the Sitwells and the walls were lined with all the great French classics . . .

These people are actually well-read! marvelled Sauge, comparing the spirited conversations at Campbell's Den with the arid exchanges of Glendrocket. Here, she felt herself to be in Europe again, whereas there, she might have been living on an unexplored planet, or even in a minefield.

At Campbell's Den, everyone worked at something, hence Lady Balquidder's acid comments about the petty bourgeoisie. Whilst the Campbells had provided their country with lawyers, surgeons and scholars, the MacFinnish clan of pirates and patricians had displayed its bloodied tartan only in the romantic Scotland of poetry and painting.

Sauge was taken out to admire the garden with its clipped yews and the flower-beds now glowing in the light of the setting sun. The bleak moors glowered jealously over this little habitation built defiantly in their midst, for Campbell's Den was even more isolated than Glendrocket.

– In October we can sometimes hear the stags, Peggy
informed her; they come to the nearby loch to drink.
Would you like to go and watch the tennis with the
others or shall we stay here?
– Oh do let's stay here, shall we? It's so nice . . .

The two young women went to sit on a bench with its back to the house. From somewhere nearby a song rose on the air, so close and so gentle it might have been the voice of the place itself.

– That's my sister, Jennifer, explained Peggy. She has a sweet voice, not very strong but very true.
– Anything stronger would be out of place, murmured Sauge quietly.

The voice rose higher, seeming to mingle with the smoke that now wisped, spiralling from one of the chimneys; the two intangibles, song and smoke, together drifted upwards, to die in the haze of the sky above. Sauge held her breath. The very soul of Scotland was revealed to her in that sweet, plaintive song and its oft-repeated themes: the endless yearnings of northern love, the longings, the fateful separations, the exile, the loneliness, the heartbreaking dignity of the Stuarts. In vain did she hope for a cry of revolt . . .

> For I and my true love
> Will never meet again,
> On the bonnie, bonnie Banks
> O' Loch Lomond.

This was the country's own refrain: bitter-sweet, passionate and resigned.

> For I and my true love
> Will never meet again . . .

A sudden, intense pain made her close her eyes for a moment.

– What's the matter? Are you all right? cried Peggy, alarmed by her pallor.
– I'm all right. I just feel a bit cold, that's all.
– We should not have sat on this bench for so long! Let's go and find the others, suggested Peggy, rising.

Very soon they came across the twins, now looking bored and sulky, all their former sparkle gone, and listlessly kicking pebbles in the drive. For a while, they had politely watched the tennis which seemed to them an effete kind of exercise. Then Mrs Campbell, seeing how little her charges were enjoying themselves, took pity on them. This had been, after all, their first real social occasion, and they had behaved beautifully. She told them to go off and do whatever they liked.

Silent and brooding, they had set off on a short walk, but after a few minutes, deprived of what had become their joint *raison d'être*, they had tacitly agreed to return to tennis and civilization, and with them, Sauge.

As they came into view, Sauge could not resist the temptation of waving her magic wand.

– Twins! she called, for this was shorter than 'Malcolm and Jean'.

Wildly they ran up to her, transformed by happiness.

God what a flirt that woman is, thought Peggy, watching the proceedings and adding, to herself: I should have said something.

CHAPTER FIVE

Since falling in love with her, the twins had never mentioned Sauge again. Each was enveloped in the preoccupied silence of love and, like workers engaged in the same task, there was no need for speech; they simply got on with the job.

The idea of adopting a more complicated approach to Sauge never occurred to them and the state of her feelings towards them presented, as they saw it, no problem. For the twins, real problems were those that required immediate attention: could Diana ever be trained into a reliable gundog; would Sauge like a ferret as a present? Would she overlook the nasty, smelly habits of such a marvellous hunting companion? Like children, they lived from day to day, united by the common bond of that miracle of creation, their faultless Sauge. They could foresee no end to this paradisiac state of affairs, though they knew she had a husband somewhere, a home and attendant obligations. These all remained very vague, however, and after delaying the date of her departure, which in turn came and then passed, Sauge made no further reference to it.

They were perfectly happy. Jean, however, was slightly more intuitive than her brother and developing fast. Apart from some painful tutoring from the local curate, she was entirely without education and her intelligence was therefore raw. She possessed an excellent memory and conveyed the totality of her thought as if pouring carefully every single drop of water from a vase. Her stories were full of details no one else would have noticed and there was something new and fresh about them, as if they had just been unwrapped for the first time. Lately, however, she had developed a new shyness which showed itself in a slight stammer. To Sauge, who noticed it, she said:

– It's as well to tune an instrument before you begin to play it.

Sauge was speechless! Jean making witty remarks, what next? Jean went on eagerly:

– I used to go to concerts, you know, when Aunt Agnes used to take us off to Edinburgh. I adore music.
– Oh, what a lovely surprise! Why didn't you tell me? cried Sauge. I only play when I think you two are well out of earshot . . .
– Oh, I've often listened to you. Malcolm, too. Haven't you, Malcolm?
– I should say! We used to hide behind the gallery curtains, so as not to disturb you. It was beautiful.
– Well we must make up for lost time, said Sauge, leading them off, arm-in-arm, towards the piano in the icy drawing-room.

There, she made the music leap out of the old piano which until her arrival had echoed only to the dignified strains of Goring-Thomas and Chaminade. When she threw herself into a spirited rendition of the Russian dance from *Petrouchka*, Malcolm could contain himself no longer. He leapt into the most complicated reel, accompanied by bloodcurdling yells. The Scots and the Russians share a wild and innate love of dancing.

– What does 'Petrouchka' mean? asked Jean as Malcolm collapsed beside her.

Sauge told them the story of the poor puppet who, being more life-like than the others, suffered the pangs of love for the sake of the wicked magician's experiments.

– I'm like Petrouchka myself, you know, said Jean, much to their astonishment.
– What? said Sauge, taken aback.
– In what way?
– I'm not sure, exactly, but I sometimes feel I am like someone else's puppet; that some stronger will than my own is telling me what to do. Then the feeling goes away and I don't think about it any more. There must be a magician in my life somewhere, don't you think? she said, then innocently, perhaps it's you.

Sauge was amazed and then suddenly overwhelmed by such distress that she could not answer. Perhaps there was some truth in Jean's naive conjectures. Partly out of vanity, and partly curiosity, Sauge had pushed her puppets as far as they could go. Knowing the secret mechanism that set them off, she had manipulated them this way and that and manoeuvred them into more and more dangerous contortions. What if it ended as in the story of Petrouchka? For she recognized that she only liked them together. They could have become a kind of music-hall turn to her: two young creatures in grease-paint dressed identically and dancing in unison . . . When they were separate the ancient Janus-like image was shattered and spoiled.

Now, every evening, Sauge played to them. It was difficult to say who was the more delighted, the twins or Lady Balquidder. The latter's brisk little being was transported back to the divine days of her youth at Bayreuth. Memories of the people and places associated with it flooded over her: Siegfried Wagner, now a somewhat flabby old gentleman with nothing god-like to him but the name; Frau Cosima, already a saint; Franz; the impassive Wotan; the Villa Wahnfried, and its *salon* crowded, as it always was, with the geniuses of the day.

One blustery night, when the drawing-room felt more icy than usual, Sauge had a sudden pang of longing, a yearning for the sun, and for the fast yet relaxed rhythm of Latin life.

– Listen, she said, seating herself at the piano. Imagine a hive-full of stars has been spilled up above, they swarm in their thousands on an indigo sky; the orange blossom is in flower again, its perfume as captivating as ever; a song of despair rises from the town as a lover's voice swoops down from the giddy heights of love . . .

And she began to play Albeniz's *Navarra*. After a few moments, she knew, without turning round, that the twins had moved closer to the piano. She felt uncomfortable. They listened so avidly that their presence became aggressive, oppressive even. As if starved, they gathered the music towards them, lapping up the notes half-formed.

Her playing suffered as a result. It quickly deteriorated into a rushing jumble of notes. Irritated, she tried to think of a way of dismissing her audience. The fireplace in this room was small and ill-suited to its size. A pathetic little fire flickered in the huge gloom.

– I feel cold, complained Sauge. Twins, do be kind and get me my shawl. I've left it in the gallery, I think.

The twins bounded off immediately. Nowhere was the shawl to be seen. They slid under the furniture, shook the cushions, and to no avail. Then Jean suddenly had the idea of looking under the dining-room table. She was rewarded, for there lay the shawl, trampled under Aunt Agnes' footstool. With a cry of triumph, Jean seized it. Hardly had she done so when Malcolm burst into the dining-room.

– I say! That's not fair! he cried indignantly. That was my idea, too! You're not going to tell her *you* found it, I hope, he threatened, his face flushed.
– Of course I am, said Jean in a little fluting voice that, in her, boded extremely ill.
– I forbid you!
– Who are you? Old Slowcoach! Old Brainless! And you want to pinch the reward from somebody more intelligent? Not likely, not this time!

93

And, hugging the shawl to herself, Jean rushed towards the door. In a bound, her brother reached it before her. Brutally he ripped the shawl from her hands and, in doing so, made a huge tear.

– See what you've done? mocked Jean, displaying the
spoiled shawl. *Now* you can tell her you found it . . . and
ripped it to shreds. Sauge *will* be pleased. Although, from
a lout like you, she shouldn't be surprised.

Malcolm was trembling with hatred and rage. He walked after her:

– Do you know why you say things like that?
– Do you know what's driving you to it?

Jean staggered back a step.

– Shall I tell you? he continued. It's jealousy. You're
jealous of us.

(*Us.* Never before used except of themselves, the word pierced her like a dagger and she blanched.)

– It's killing you, isn't it? And what do you expect, you
poor girl? You're jealous, not only of your cousin,
because she's a real woman and you're just a tomboy but
you're jealous of your brother, too!

With a barely human cry, Jean flung herself on her brother, for he it was who had just revealed the reason for her own unhappiness. Taken by surprise, he stumbled backwards, lost his balance and fell full length on the floor, dragging his sister with him. His head hit the square foot of the mahogany table. A trickle of blood appeared on his left temple.

– Oh! cried Jean, drawing away in fright. I've killed
Malcolm!

Tears started in her eyes. She had killed the very person she loved best in the whole world!

– Malcolm, my darling Malcolm, speak to me! Say
you're not dead . . .

Not a word. Aghast, Jean got up, pushed back her damp
curls and ran towards the drawing-room, towards light and
the world of reason.

– Sauge! Sauge! I've killed Malcolm. I've killed Malcolm,
Sauge!

It was Sauge who appeared first, looking very pale. She
had almost expected these cries; the distraught expression,
the wild hair, yes, yes, she had foreseen it all. Hesitantly, she
stepped forward.

Malcolm was not dead, however. He developed a fever
and had to remain in bed for a few days, but his wound was
superficial. Jean, in whom something seemed to have been
snuffed out, paced nervously back and forth in his bedroom.
In the last few days, she had become almost ugly. Malcolm,
in contrast, had never looked so handsome. How could
Sauge have imagined them to look alike? All she saw at the
moment was the beautiful virile serenity of Malcolm, con-
trasting with Jean's absurd anxiety. It was odd how this
accident had helped to define them and to situate each of
them separately . . .

For Malcolm, too, everything had changed. He fell as a
boy and rose a man. The incident that triggered off the fall
seemed trivial and irrelevant to him now. How he would
laugh about it later with Jean. He made a face and winked at
her, to try and show his affection. Either from modesty or
out of rancour, Jean affected not to notice. The fact was that,
of the three, she alone remained unchanged.

In Malcolm's little bedroom, high at the top of a turret next
to the dovecote, an uncomfortable silence reigned. It was
broken only by the sound of pigeons' wings beating as they
took dustbaths in the eavestroughs outside. One small

window opposite the bed framed Ben Lomond, as gentle and distant as an old man's gaze. From the other, all that was visible was the dark band of pines, a frown on the brow of the moors . . .

The room was perched so high up that it felt like a lighthouse against which birds of the night, like giant moths, would fling themselves. There was a disconcerting mixture of child and man in the objects within. Why the pipes with the packets of sweets? By what miracle had that ten-year-old's trumpet survived, lying comfortably now against two pistols? Animals followed Malcolm wherever he went, even into his room. Here, a stuffed weasel, dispatcher of many hundreds of rabbits, occupied a place of honour on the desk, where never a letter was penned. The horseshoes of various defunct ponies were lined up on the mantelpiece beneath a flourish of crops and whips.

One photograph, and one only, hung above the bed. It was of his mother, a little before her death. In it, the splendour of her hair contrasted vividly with the apathetic face beneath, from which all trace of happiness had fled. The hair seemed to burst forth in a wild, independent profusion, like weeds on a grave . . . The pale, anaemic picture was in marked contrast to the splendid body lying under its protection. Sauge's gaze travelled from one to the other. Malcolm in bed! What condescension! Still, its wood had once been a tree, and the wool of its quilts once a sheep . . .

Suddenly, Jean, who had been looking out of the window, leaned over her brother to see if he was asleep. One above, one below; Jean seemed to look down into waters reflecting her own image. Sauge turned away. She felt ill-at-ease in this beastly den; she was troubled by the inviolable purity of this couple and by their colossal intimacy . . . She might have said something, seeing that her brother was not asleep, but no! there she was, returning to her post. Oh, the eternal gazing.

Jean felt a similar irritation, intensified by the presence of another female in the room which had hitherto known herself alone. She drummed her fingers against the glass, hoping the other would leave. The antics of the pigeons provided some distraction; Jean made up stories about them.

– Look! she gasped, that one for example, oh the poor thing, he's lost all his feathers!

Her brother pretended not to hear. With a little encouragement she would come and sit on the bed. Why didn't she go away now she knew he was going to be all right! Malcolm longed to be alone with Sauge; in the strongly medicated atmosphere of the room he faintly sensed her perfume.

Night had begun to fall quickly now; from seven onwards, the lawns were covered with mist that crept up as far as the low mountain slopes . . . The high and airy room felt insubstantial, unconstrained; it had become a kite, a soap-bubble and, light as a feather, it seemed to drift through the air and into space. Sauge savoured the feeling of being outside time, and beyond the reach of anyone or anything. The spell was broken by Jean who, sensing that, at whatever cost, this silence must be broken, announced in a peremptory voice that she was going to feed the dogs.

– Yes, do, murmured Malcolm, his head buried in the pillows. She walked hesitantly away, wheeled suddenly round, then left the room, whistling a defiant little tune as she went.

It was as if her continued presence had been keeping out the dusk. As she left, it engulfed the room, swallowing up the last vestiges of light remaining within. There was no one in the whole wide world save Malcolm now, and Sauge.

– Do you . . . do you need anything? she asked, so that he should not hear the thudding of her heart.
– Nothing, thank you.

Was there a hint of irony in that muffled voice?

– In that case, I'll leave you in peace.

The tremor in her voice showed how close was the danger.

– Are you going? asked Malcolm, now only visible as a dark patch on the pillow.

Sauge's heart lurched. She leaned for a moment against the bed. Oh to take him in her arms! To speak the wild desperate words he had never heard! To smother with her own kisses that face that had known only a grandmother's and a sister's. She stumbled gratefully to the lamp at the head of his bed and switched it on. Clear, pitiless light flooded over them as Malcolm, instinctively, put his hand to his eyes.

– Oh sorry, stammered Sauge, sorry!

She was saved yet again.

Jean's real torture began only when Malcolm was up and about again. Then, for the first time, she did indeed feel *de trop*. It was on Sauge's arm that Malcolm leaned; Sauge it was who read to him when he had a headache; and it was Sauge too, who took his favourite spaniel, Atalanta, for her walks.

But far from being hostile to Jean, Sauge was at pains to show her every consideration; she showered her with attentions and little kindnesses. Feeling vaguely guilty, she wanted to do all in her power to repair the damage she had caused and which continued to fill her with pain and remorse.

Jean, torn between two fateful and closely interwoven loves, began to feel like Sauge and Malcolm's child. There were days when she made no resistance to it, and these were full of a sweet melancholy that matched the onset of autumn with its daily mists. A mist formed too, between her and the others, relegating her to a different dimension, without relief and without perspective . . .

From time to time, she returned to her only friend; old Mrs Bracken, as constant as her knick-knacks and her clocks. In the small, fossilized room, Jean's large, stooping figure, always dressed in unconsciously flattering fawns, looked enormously out of place. Tearing her hat off as she entered, she settled heavily in a horsehair .armchair and stretched out her muscular legs. Opposite her, dressed in respectable black alpaca, sat Mrs Bracken. She waited for Jean to relax and talk:

– So good to be at your house. Nice and peaceful here.
– Do you think so, Miss Jean?
– Oh yes. Much nicer than up at the castle.

Mrs Bracken could not take this seriously. To her way of thinking, nothing could be more splendid than Glendrocket.

Tick, tock . . . tick, tock . . ., the grandfather clock filled in any lapses in the conversation. Silently, Mrs Bracken offered Jean a packet of the famous humbugs she loved so much. She took two, automatically, and her cheeks swelled into a cherub's. The mint-filled silence, punctuated only by the ticking of the clock, was finally broken by the mistress of the house.

– I saw Mr Malcolm pass earlier on. He was on his way
to Macgregor's farm.
– Ah? Was my cousin with him?
– Yes indeed, she popped in for a chat. She's certainly not
proud, that lass. We all love her here. The Master and I
think the world of her!

Very rarely did Mrs Bracken offer such confidences and, as always, Jean was torn between two emotions. She was glad of her cousin's popularity but sorry that she was now so regularly associated with her own dear brother. They lapsed into silence again. The old lady contemplated Jean's relaxed beauty, spread out before her like some glorious crop ready to be harvested; she seemed to belong to an essentially earthy breed with sparkling wine for blood in its veins.

Pity, thought Mrs Bracken. Pity there aren't more young men hereabouts.

– How do you think my brother looks?
– Mr Malcolm always looks healthy, even when he's not
very well.
– That's true. Jean sighed deeply. I do too. I mean, for
example, I haven't slept for ages but you'd never know,
to look at me. It's ridiculous, she concluded angrily.

If I didn't know her, I'd say this young lady had had a
disappointment in love, thought the old retainer, but was
wise enough to hold her tongue.

– I hate the way I look, went on the young woman. All
I'll ever be is a poor substitute for Malcolm.

So she's angry with Sir Malcolm, but why? and who's at
the bottom of it? wondered Mrs Bracken, amazed.

– You know those awful doubles that actors use when
they're ill, asked Jean, inspired by her own anger. Well,
I'll never settle for being one of them. I'd rather be . . .

Here she stopped abruptly. Mrs Bracken was seriously
worried now. This kind of talk reminded her of the despair-
ing monologues of Jean's mother, who had spent her life
wishing only for death.

– I mean, if they only needed me, she went on. But you
can see they don't. They get on fine without me.
– Who's this 'they'?
– Why, my brother and my cousin, of course.
– Ah!

Mrs Bracken understood at last. Her first impulse was to
say 'Is that all?' Then she realized how intense was the grief
at the root of this *cri de coeur* and pitied the poor girl with all
her heart. With no mother, no friends and no lovers, it was
natural that her brother should mean everything to her. His
being taken over by an attractive stranger would obviously
make her apprehensive. To console her, the old lady said:

– Don't worry, Miss Jean. Your cousin isn't here for ever; she'll be going away soon and then Mr Malcolm will need you more than ever.

However, this failed to cheer Jean, who grew gloomier still. Painfully she uttered the words:

– I don't want her to go. I don't know what it is that I want.

Meanwhile, Sauge's husband, Alain, had been preparing his *coup d'état*. Her letters, growing increasingly rare and evasive, had confirmed his worst suspicions. It must be a love-affair that was keeping her in Scotland. He had stopped replying to her letters, considering it a useless farce; besides, knowing her, he judged silence to be more effective than words. But the moment had come to act. Desperate situations call for desperate measures, and her absence for two months, instead of the planned one, was tantamount to desertion. With a pounding heart, he drafted a wire:

URGENTLY ADVISE YOU SPEND WINTER GLENDROCKET STOP
LEAVING MARSEILLES TUESDAY

Fearful that his plan would not work, he went to bed dead-drunk that night; this was something he had not done since that business in Budapest . . .

Alain's plan was obviously working and his unbroken silence beginning to take effect at last. Though she tried to banish it to the furthest recesses of her mind, Sauge was prey to constant unease. It was nothing serious, of course, but under the show of confidence, and the fluctuations of her more immediate feelings, its low whimper could always be heard. Around her principal emotional structure she had built smaller, temporary shrines which in no way detracted from its importance. The more she felt attracted to others, the more she needed Alain. And now, the very foundation of her existence, the cornerstone on which her entire, complicated life had lain, was threatening to disintegrate. This was by no means the first time Alain had jibbed; with an unexpected buck he had unseated his rider before now, but, this time, would she be able to catch up with him? Perhaps, on this occasion, she had let things go too far. Was he in love with somebody else? As usual, she had to admit that only when eaten up by jealousy did she become genuinely, sharply alive. Only jealousy reached her vital parts. The other, passing preoccupations that engaged her from time to time were mere curtain-raisers for this, the real drama. She likened herself to a bull, waiting for the *coup d'espada* to die. Panic-stricken, she drafted the telegram she had planned to send the previous month and this time sent it . . .

With the clear-sightedness that imminent disaster produces in human beings, she saw that Alain was indispensable to her, whilst the others were only a temporary luxury; pretty decorations which she should discard should they threaten the equilibrium of her existence . . . A little calmer by now, she began to *tidy* her emotions. The moment had come to work her way out of the labyrinth she had so determinedly entered.

Did she love Malcolm? Yes, if she could keep Alain; no if she had to lose him. What did she mean, moreover, by love? Malcolm, young, handsome and totally submissive to her, could never be more than a page in her life, a peripheral kind of person, charming but superfluous. Symbolizing a devoted conquest, his arms might occupy a respectable though hardly legendary quarter of the family escutcheon.

This situation could never have arisen outside Scotland. Wild Caledonia, with its heather heaths and fogs, nurtures such illusions: certitudes become ephemera, one's beliefs crumble. Every visitor to Scotland is potentially gullible. Sauge, in her mind's eye already half-way back to Alain, turned on the twins the searchlight of lucidity.

The tensions in the balance of the situation reminded her of the moment when, in ballet, two dancers follow the *première danseuse* and bring her back on stage. With hindsight, she saw that without Alain she would never be happy with Malcolm and that, if she had to abandon one or the other, her choice was already made.

Eager to have it over and done with, she went to look for Malcolm. By a stroke of good luck, for she was afraid Jean might remonstrate, she found him alone in the 'arsenal' tying flies. These flies were little works of art in themselves, requiring extraordinary patience and application to make. As he saw her come in, he put down the finch's feather which he was just about to tie in with that of a jay and pulled up the only comfortable chair. A *tête-à-tête!* He was smiling already at the thought of this heaven-sent encounter. Sauge knew she had not a minute to lose; that she had to attack while the thought of Alain was still fresh in her mind:

– Listen, Malcolm, dear. You've got to be reasonable
about this. I'm going to have to leave. And this time it's
definite.

Malcolm's expression changed. Incredulity turned to anger. She must not give him time to think. Quickly, she improvised:

– My husband is ill. I have to leave as soon as possible.
– That's not true! I don't believe you. Malcolm's huge
voice crushed her words like so many ants. If it was true,
he continued implacably, you would have told me
straight away, when you got the telegram, instead of two
hours later!
– Very well, you're right, it's not true, Sauge confessed,
turning to the truth in blind fury. It's worse than that.
My husband is threatening to leave me if I don't go back.

Before she had time to say another word, Malcolm took her in his arms and, madly kissing her neck and her hair, muttered in a broken voice:

– I love you, I love you! You can't leave; I love you. I
can't lose you now. I can only live near you! Your
husband can ask for a divorce and I shall marry you!

These last words were uttered in the presence of Jean who, on hearing voices, had rushed in. Seeing Malcolm and Sauge locked in an embrace, she paled, stifled a little cry and had to lean for a moment against the wall.

Malcolm and Sauge looked at her, paralysed with guilt and clinging to each other for mutual protection. With this picture etched in her mind for ever, Jean pushed open the door and disappeared.

Sauge disengaged herself easily. Malcolm's thoughts, as well as her own, were now on Jean alone.

– Malcolm, did you see her face? We must go after her!

Malcolm shrugged.

– What's the point?
– Oh Malcolm, you poor fool! You've got no intuition. It's precisely because she was afraid we *would* leave her alone that she's run away!
– Rubbish. She knows perfectly well we'd never abandon her. She knows she'd have come to live with us.
– Listen, my friend. If you'd just given me time, I'd have said straight away the whole thing was impossible. Unfortunately, Jean heard you but she didn't know what my reply would have been. She's forgotten I'm married and that you're too young to marry anybody and she's thinking of it as a *fait accompli*. She sees us united for life, leaving her to the tender mercies of Aunt Agnes while we swan around the world together.
– She should know me better than that.

Malcolm had tears in his eyes.

– Oh Malcolm, dear, Jean may be only a child in some respects but she loves us and she's suffering terribly. She can see both further and not so far as we do at the moment and, like all children, she thinks maybe a temporary situation is going to last for ever. We must go and find her as quickly as we can.

It was as if a force outside herself had taken charge of Sauge's personality. Never, in all the time she had been in Scotland, had she felt so sure of her actions. Malcolm needed no second bidding. It was obvious that his sister was uppermost in his mind. Sometimes it takes a real cataclysm to clarify emotional priorities.

– I'll go to Pixies' Pool, cried Malcolm, in the courtyard already. You'd better take the road up to the moors!

With a heavy heart, Sauge went the way he suggested. She imagined she could hear again the refrain that had moved her so deeply at the Campbells':

> Ye'll tak the high road,
> And I'll tak the low,
> And I'll be in Scotland before ye,
> For me and my true love
> We'll never meet again,
> On the bonnie, bonnie
> Banks of Loch Lomond.

The theme of Scotland itself: frustrated love, hopeless separation. Sauge was engulfed by an almost unbearable sadness. It was a feeling of having sullied her life with all sorts of artificial stimulants and contaminants to its purity. The air smelt of rain and as she walked quickly ahead, the occasional fox-coloured leaf floated earthwards. The sky was swollen with clouds; like enormous baroque pearls they proceeded majestically by . . . Yes, she had sullied her life and the Scottish blood within it which should have run clear and slow. Like the waters of the Stole nearby, with its thousands of wildly darting fish, it should contain thoughts and ideas that flashed within, sometimes struggling against the current . . .

Could Jean have come this way? She called her name repeatedly. A blackbird pecking the red berries off a rowan bush flew away, chattering. Sauge's voice was drowned in the noise of the water. There is nothing more desolate than a voice crying in the wilderness. Sauge shuddered and her anxiety grew pressing and sharp. She was convinced that everything was taking place according to some prearranged plan. These empty cries had been heard before, but where? In what kind of limbo? Anxious to *know*, she took the little path leading onto the moors. Here, everything was quiet and she missed the sound of the water. The mountains looming over the moors looked like spectators comfortably seated and waiting for the curtain to rise . . . She knew with utter certainty that she was one of the actors; that she was, perhaps, unknowingly, already on stage. Before her, the moors stretched out of sight, giving the impression of an empty space within which it would be easy to search. Walking was difficult, however, and dense little clumps of brown heather got in her way and slowed her down. Elsewhere, she slithered in marshy patches where unseen pools lay hidden beneath the moss. From time to time her sad, solitary call rang out:

– Jean! Jean! Where are you, Jean?

'This day was suspended between two ordinary days.' Where had she heard that phrase? It was so apt for today. 'Between two ordinary days', this day of crucifixion . . . was this a premonition or just one of the many absurd thoughts to which any exhausted mind is prey? In her nervousness, she longed for a storm of some kind, an earthquake even, to calm or to distract her. There was not even a wind. She loved wind and storm and when as a child she was asked if she was afraid, the answer was:

– No, I have a nest in the wind!

She had been determined to continue looking as far as the loch but suddenly her courage failed, and her legs refused to carry her a single step further. Nightmarishly, she saw herself as a general, viewing the battle from a distance; emissaries, arriving with bad news, galloped, reins flapping along the skyline. With the dust of the journey still upon them, they leapt off their horses and flung themselves at her feet: 'He is vanquished! We have left him covered in blood on the field of battle . . .' With this, the song of Scotland, taken up by a thousand voices, rose up in glorious despair:

> For me and my true love
> We'll never meet again . . .

I feel somehow amputated, thought Sauge. I should have lost consciousness but my little brain is continuing to function.

She begun to retrace her steps. From that moment onwards, nothing was surprising to her, and her faculties seemed to be endowed with unusual energy. She walked back with a brisk, almost confident step. The wind had now risen, blowing in gusts and lifting the leaves with their pale undersides into full view . . .

Still without emotion, she registered considerable activity within the castle. Maids were running agitatedly in and out. Macgregor and another gamekeeper were speaking in low voices at the angle of the gunroom. With a light step still, she crossed the courtyard and entered the great arched hall with its antlers and its coats-of-arms.

Here it was that she saw Malcolm, bent over the lifeless body of his sister and holding her still in his arms. Water was streaming everywhere, momentarily restoring to the flagstones their original hue.

Brother and sister formed a strangely harmonious *Pietà* that might have been carved from the same block of stone. What now lay before her eyes was the old terror made real; the nightmare made tangible at last. In the distance, at the other end of the hall, Lady Balquidder sobbed; with difficulty, as it was twenty years since last she had wept.

Sauge was conscious of all these things with the detachment of one whose anguished body sends its spirit on ahead, to reconnoitre. Instinctively, she raised a hand to protect herself. Part of her attention was engaged in the most banal thoughts: Malcolm should go and change immediately; Lady Balquidder's sobs sounded exactly like her old pony Sinbad's asthma.

Suddenly her heart turned over, plunging into blackness and chaos. If he looks at me, she thought, I shall die. Malcolm, however, was incapable of movement. Soon he was bound to lift his head! Oh to flee before he saw her!

Malcolm's hair mingled with Jean's, hers entwined with wisps of grass. Her face was buried in her brother's shoulder and one of her arms hung down like a vine uprooted. Her whole long body lay in an easy abandonment, sinister now with the sharp angles of life removed.

And then the thing she had most dreaded happened. Gently, very gently, taking infinite care, and as if fearing to wake her, he lifted his head away. Sauge's heart almost stopped beating. Malcolm's hallucinating gaze reached her. The eyes widened in incredulity. Several moments elapsed before comprehension turned to rage and accusation:

– What are you doing here? he asked, his hoarse voice
barely recognizable. Haven't you had enough? You've
killed my sister. You've broken my heart. I should have
thought that would do. We were happy. We didn't need
anybody. Then you crept in, with your beautiful,
insinuating ways and, little by little, you poisoned us . . .
Yet she loved you. She loved only you and me! We've
killed her. He grew pale and began to tremble. You had
better leave now unless you want me to strangle you with
my bare hands. Go! he shouted, go! as if this was the only
word left in the world.

Sauge started. None of Malcolm's threats had touched her. None could pierce the dull resignation she felt towards anything that could happen now that Jean was dead. Only the unexpected sound of his voice showed her she must now gather all her silent, fleeting thoughts and leave.

Holding his terrible yet precious gaze, for she loved him

and knew she would see him no more, Sauge retreated, feeling her way along the walls, and out. Around the twins, silence fell, broken only by a small sound, discreet and monotonous in its regularity. Lady Balquidder sobbed . . .